NOBLE FA

From Kansas to OZ

NOBLE FAMILY CHRONICLES BOOK I

From Kansas to OZ

A Novel by

Gail Larson

WINEPRESS WP PUBLISHING

© 2006 by Gail Larson. All rights reserved

WinePress Publishing (PO Box 428, Enumclaw, WA 98022) functions only as book publisher. As such, the ultimate design, content, editorial accuracy, and views expressed or implied in this work are those of the author.

No part of this publication may be reproduced, stored in a retrieval system or transmitted in any way by any means—electronic, mechanical, photocopy, recording or otherwise—without the prior permission of the copyright holder, except as provided by USA copyright law.

Unless otherwise noted, all Scriptures are taken from the Holy Bible, New International Version, Copyright © 1973, 1978, 1984 by the International Bible Society. Used by permission of Zondervan Publishing House. The "NIV" and "New International Version" trademarks are registered in the United States Patent and Trademark Office by International Bible Society.

Scripture references marked KJV are taken from the King James Version of the Bible.

Scripture references marked NASB are taken from the New American Standard Bible, © 1960, 1963, 1968, 1971, 1972, 1973, 1975, 1977 by The Lockman Foundation. Used by permission.

ISBN 1-57921-853-9
Library of Congress Catalog Card Number: 2005905969

Dedication

Dedicated to Mom and Dad—the Cavalry
and
To the Following Travelers
Who Have Already Reached Oz:

Charles Eldon Hilstad
Lori Beth Hilstad Daane
C. J. Hovick
Douglas David Marshall
Francis Arnold Sanford
Jessie Arvilla Satter Sanford

Table of Contents

Acknowledgments — ix
Prologue — xi

1. The Cyclone — 15
2. Council with the Munchkins — 23
3. How Dorothy Saved the Scarecrow — 31
4. The Road Through the Forest — 41
5. The Rescue of the Tin Woodman — 47
6. The Cowardly Lion — 55
7. The Journey to the Great Oz — 63
8. The Deadly Poppy Fields — 69
9. The Queen of the Field Mice — 77
10. The Guardian of the Gates — 83
11. The Emerald City of Oz — 89
12. The Search for the Wicked Witch — 95
13. The Rescue — 103
14. The Winged Monkeys — 111
15. The Discovery of Oz the Terrible — 119
16. The Magic Art of the Great Humbug — 127
17. How the Balloon Was Launched — 135
18. Away to the South — 143

19. Attacked by the Fighting Trees	149
20. The Dainty China Country	157
21. The Lion Becomes the King of Beasts	163
22. The Country of the Quadlings	169
23. Glinda Grants Dorothy's Wish	175
24. Home Again	179
About the Author	185

Acknowledgments

Until the journey through an extended illness becomes personal, most earthly travelers feel no compulsion to explore the depths of daily challenges caused by ill health.

It is for this reason that I am grateful to several people who have shared their insight and emotional journeys while traveling the road of extended illness. They are: Susie Middlebrooks, Carol Thomas, Pat Roberts, Libby White, Janet Mansfield, Anne Cassler, Patsy Erdman, and Marian Clakley. Thank you also to the hospital patients, clinic outpatients, and home-health patients for whom I have had the privilege of caring through twenty-seven years of nursing.

Thank you also to Athena Dean and her team at WinePress Publishing for sharing their professional expertise and for understanding the message of this manuscript. Thanks to Kathy Ide, my editor, for her unending patience and encouragement as I continue to learn. I am deeply indebted to the Larson Ministries team: Susie, Jen, Bonnie, Terri, Kathy, Beverly, for their encouragement, support, and unwavering belief in this project. Special thanks go to Teri Miller for "birthing" the "My Oasis Bag" project. Also my thanks go to Vicar Ed Obermueller for his vision for the original book's cover. To Paulette Schliep, heartfelt thanks for my daily front-door surprises. Thanks also to Patsy Lewis for walking me through the valley on a day we will remember as long as we draw breath.

And of course, thanks to my family, for standing by my side as I learned how to pack my bags with enough hope to travel through my own journey with breast cancer.

Finally, to our Savior and Lord, I lift my thanks with every fiber of my being. This is Your book, Father. Thank You for giving me the words to share and the courage to write them. I am humbled and awed by Your involvement in my life. May You use this manuscript in any way You see fit.

—Gail Larson

Prologue

Dark clouds hovered overhead. Mr. Gumpy stopped the car. He jumped out, put up the top, and down came the rain. The road grew muddier and muddier, and the wheels began to spin. Mr. Gumpy looked at the hill ahead. "Some of you will have to get out and push," he said.[1]

Whether you are driving along the muddy roads of an extended illness or pushing a family member up its slippery slope, the way can seem torturous, blinding, and exhausting as rain clouds empty their watery load on your head.

In my journey, the first raindrop hit my forehead on the morning of my sister's forty-fourth birthday, February 2, 1999. In the semi-darkness of dawn, with my eyes closed, I methodically completed the steps of my monthly self-breast exam. As a registered nurse, I knew the importance of the regular checks and seldom postponed performing them past the first few days of each month.

Right side, clean as a whistle. Left side, *not!*

---

[1] John Burningham, "Mr. Gumpy's Motor Car," *The World Treasury of Children's Literature: Book Two* (Clifton Fadiman: Little, Brown and Company, 1984).

My eyes flew open in shock as my nursing brain took over and had the following dialogue with my personal-life brain:

> Nurse brain: Don't panic. Statistics show most lumps are merely cysts.
> Personal brain: But I've never had a cyst.
> Nurse brain: Maybe you've developed one. After all, you're older than you used to be.
> Personal brain: Not that much older! I can't believe I didn't find this last month.
> Nurse brain: Maybe it wasn't there last month.
> Personal brain: Wasn't there? That means it's fast-growing.
> Nurse brain: Why don't you find out what it is?
> Personal brain: What if it's cancer?
> Nurse brain: It might be. But you won't know if you don't get out of bed, pick up the phone, make an appointment, and find out.
> Personal brain: That is a very wise idea. I had better do that now.

And so began another story of another woman who found a lump in her breast, except this time the woman was me. I had reached the young-old age of forty-eight. I had more than twenty-five years of experience as a nurse and had recently changed careers. I was thrilled to be working full time as minister of music and worship at our family's church. My new job felt "right" and I was convinced God had clearly led me into it. I began the job with all the vigor and enthusiasm of a kid at Christmas and I didn't think life could be any brighter.

Until I discovered the lump. With my nursing background, jumping through the hoops of the health care system seemed as natural as breathing. But when the tests revealed the lump as cancerous, breathing didn't come so easily anymore. Treatment was radical and aggressive, with surgeries and chemotherapy.

At one point during the journey, a sympathetic friend struggled with the seemingly unfair nature of God. I remember this person asking me, "Why would He let you, of all people, be hit with this awful disease, when you are so clearly doing His work, His way, in His church?"

Having spent a great deal of time in waiting rooms over the past months, I was able to answer my friend, "Why not me? I'm no different from anyone else. God is God. If He allows this disease to come into my life, I do not have to agonize about it, because I am His child, and He loves me. I know that for a fact. In one way or another, everything will be okay."

And in one way or another, everything is. In fact, it's better than okay.

The journey led me uphill, downhill, and around curves. A couple of times I found myself with a dead battery and stuck in a busy intersection with oncoming traffic. Sometimes it rained gently while other times my legs nearly buckled under the weight of the water pouring down on my head. And often the sun shined brightly but I didn't have the energy to open the curtains and let the light inside.

However, because I knew God was not only traveling beside me, but was also in front of me, behind me, and below me, I continued to travel *through* the illness.

This is not the usual "have faith in God and everything will be fine" story. Sometimes life brings us to a turning point and we realize that even though we have faith in God, everything will *not* be fine when measured by earthly standards.

On an unexpected "walk through the valley" one day, I experienced a depth of His presence I had never known. As I lay on a table in the emergency room, with life literally bleeding out of me, I comprehended that I was not alone. God surrounded me in such a tangible way that I still have moments where I ache for the feeling, the bigger-than-peace sensation that I experienced that day. Now I possess a glimpse of what Paul meant when he said, "For me, to live is Christ and to die is gain" (Philippians 1:21 NIV).

So I urge you, dear reader, to keep your head up and your heart wide open as you journey through the pages of this book. God will use these words to help you up a steep mountain, down a muddy hill, or across a busy intersection.

I know this for a fact.

Because it is the reason I am still here.

To tell the story—His story—His way. Each chapter begins with a summary of the events in the *Wizard of Oz*[2] and continues with the diary entries of three fictional characters. Although these people live only in my imagination, their personalities were compiled from decades of observing and interacting with men and women across the country who have struggled with illness. Following each chapter is "Something to Think About"—my personal thoughts and experiences with this disease called cancer.

Let's begin, shall we? It can be a long trip from Kansas to Oz.

---

[2] L. Frank Baum's *The Wonderful Wizard of Oz* and its many sequels were originally published in the early 1900s.

CHAPTER ONE

The Cyclone

A young girl named Dorothy lived with her Uncle Henry, Aunt Em, and a small black dog named Toto in the middle of the great, gray Kansas prairies. One day the sky became grayer than usual and a cyclone hit the house. Strong winds carried it for miles, with Dorothy and Toto trapped inside it. Dorothy felt lonely and afraid. She wondered if she would be broken to pieces when the house fell from the sky. After hours passed and nothing happened, she resolved to wait calmly and see what the future would bring. In spite of the airborne house and wailing wind, she closed her eyes and took a nap.

There is a place inside every cyclone where the winds are still, where the mind is at rest, and where God grasps the heart.

"Strength! Courage! Don't be timid; don't get discouraged. God, your God, is with you every step you take."
—Joshua 1:9

Louis, a married man in his retirement years, with three grown children, writes...

Dear Lord,

I had this urge to write "Dear diary," but that seemed too foolish. A diary can't hear me or acknowledge my existence. You, on the other hand, are supposed to always be here for me, always hear me, always know the solutions to my problems. I'm not sure I believe all that, but it's what I've been told for most of my life.

I guess if You already know everything I don't have to tell You, but I need to write down the events of these past days. Maybe I can make sense of them if I see it on paper. Maybe I'll be able to figure out what is happening to me.

My wife, Jan, finally talked me into doing something about this cough I've had for most of the winter. It really hasn't been bothering me much…it's just a small dry cough now and then. I didn't see the point of seeing a doctor. He'd only give me a prescription for some antibiotics and I hate using that stuff. Upsets my stomach. And I hear if you take too much of it, your body builds up resistance against it and it doesn't work anymore.

But Jan kept pushing me so I went to see that young Doc McNeil. He's okay—not a bad doctor for being only thirty-five years old. I figured he could handle a simple cough. Nothing too complicated about that. I always saw his dad, Old Doc McNeil, till he retired five years ago and left his practice to the son.

Anyway, the doc listened to my cough, took some pictures of my chest, held them up to the light, and said we'd need to do more tests. I don't know how he figured that out. All he did was hold up a black film to the light. I couldn't see a thing on it. But the next morning, I was flat on my back looking up at a bright light in the ceiling.

The nurse sprayed some stuff in my throat and the whole inside of my mouth went numb—even my tongue. Horrible sensation. Not to be able to feel my teeth or control my spit was awful. Then Doc started pushing a three-foot black tube down my throat. I fought it every inch of the way.

The Cyclone

I gagged and coughed and choked till tears ran down my cheeks. At one point I sat straight up and they had to push me back down. I could feel that tube sliding past my vocal cords. Felt like the ridges on those rhythm sticks you play in music class in elementary school. But once it got down there, it wasn't painful or even very uncomfortable.

I guess Doc did what he needed to do in there. He took samples of what he saw. After it was over, my body shook like crazy, as if I were freezing cold. They piled blankets on me, but nothing helped. The shaking finally passed and the whole thing was done.

That was six days ago. Yesterday, the phone call came. I knew I was in trouble when I heard the doc's voice because he lets his nurses talk to people if it's no big deal.

I have a tumor. It's malignant—the kind that spreads. I hate to say the other word because it makes me feel sicker than I am. And I'm really not that sick. Just have a little cough. I wish I hadn't gone to see the doc. Probably should have taken more Vicks cough syrup.

Now I have to start a "therapy regime," he says. Therapy regime, my eye! He's talking about that chemo poison. Shooting up my body with poison doesn't seem like therapy to me.

No guarantees, he said.

So, Lord, I'm praying to You. I know I haven't been as close to You as I probably should have been and I'm really sorry about that. But if You could see Your way clear to help me through this mess, I'd be glad to go back to church and help Your work along.

I'm seventy-one years old. I know You take people home who are my age, but I figure I have ten good years left in me. I'd kind of like to get to know my kids a little better. With them all grown and gone and busy with their own lives, I've tried to stay out of their business.

I remember how I hated it when my dad tried to run my life for me. But now I'm thinking I'd like to see what kind of people my kids turned into, and maybe…just maybe…they'll see that I care about them. Never was able to say it out loud. Maybe You could help me with that part of it too.

      Guess that's it for now.
      Suppose it's time to say the "amen."
      Amen.

Trisha, a middle-aged wife and mother, writes…

Lord God,

What are You thinking? I'm a wife. A mom. A nurse. And I'm only forty-two years old. Pardon me, but I think You've lost Your holy mind! Surely You don't expect me to sit down and swallow this without a fight, do You? Or is that Your objective? Are You trying to teach me patience or courage?

Whatever it is, I'm sure I can learn some other way. I don't have time for this craziness. My child needs my full attention. My husband doesn't cook. What possessed You to let this happen to me?

I had myself convinced it was only a cyst. According to the research, most lumps are. I decided right away I wasn't going to be one of those hysterical women who lose all control when they find a lump on their breast. And the plan was working, too, because I calmly went through the steps to get it diagnosed. I'm a nurse, after all. I know the system. People do this every day. *It's no big deal.*

I saw the ob-gyn doctor first. He decided I needed more mammogram views. So I went. The radiologist recommended an ultrasound. I had that done as well. They put the films in my hand and told me to take them to an "expert" who would read the results.

I drove straight to the "expert's" office. But when I pulled into the parking lot, I opened the films myself and held them up to the light through the car window. Who wouldn't be curious enough to open the envelope and look at their own films?

I'm no expert, but I've seen enough films in twenty years of nursing to tell something was definitely there. My saliva dried up when I identified the area in question. I stuffed the films back into the manila envelope, grabbed my purse, and stepped out of the car to see the "expert."

As I walked across the parking lot, I thought about how fast life can change. A week ago, my biggest challenge was getting Steven picked up from soccer practice on the days I worked. And now, this pregnant black cloud of doom hung over my head, ready to explode.

I walked down the hall to the "expert's" office. The sign read, "Suite 104, Dr. Jonathan M. Leverman, Cancer Surgeon."

Cancer Surgeon? That chicken-hearted radiologist! If he was so sure the density on the film was cancerous, he should have told me. How cruel to let a patient find out this kind of news while standing in a cold, clinical hallway, all alone, with the word *cancer* jumping off the wall at her. At *me*.

Of course, I knew there was a possibility of cancer. But did they have to send me off with a smile on their faces to the next office to find out? Whatever happened to honesty? Whatever happened to preparation? Whatever happened to calm explanations? They need to let nurses run the health care system. We wouldn't allow something like this to happen.

Lord God Almighty. *Cancer*. I'm stunned. I've done my best to be Your child through my life. I've been baptized. I've been confirmed. I married someone of the same faith. We seldom miss attending church. We pray at mealtimes and bedtime. Once a week we gather after supper and read Your Word. What more do You want?

Can't You do me a favor and make this go away? Or has my entire life been a preparation for this one big test?

No answer.

I guess that's it then. I have to open this door, walk up to the sign-in desk, smile at the secretary, and sign my name. I have to sit down on the ugly paisley love seat over on the far wall, flip through the pages of a magazine, and pretend to be rational until the nurse calls my name. What I'd really like to do is charge into the office and scream, "Get this thing out of me!"

I imagine the next step will be the Big Biopsy. I'm going to tell the "expert" cancer surgeon, the honorable Dr. Jonathan M. Leverman, to take wide margins and cut the whole thing out so I can be done with it. With any luck at all, I'll be finished by the end of the week and will only have to deal with some localized soreness.

Well, I'll say this for You, Lord—You are certainly full of surprises.

I'm not going to say "amen" right now because I know I'm not finished with You yet.

Luke, a young boy, writes…

Hi, Jesus.

I been tired a lot lately. Mom says the docter will help me. We went to see him today. He didn't help me. He hurt me.

He stuck a needle in my arm and took out some blood. Mom says it will help him figger out what he needs to do to make me better. I'm still tired. And now my arm hurts where he put the needle.

Will You pleese help me? My legs feel heavy. I can't run fast when I feel like this. I wanna play soccer with the guys. They need me on the teem. But all I feel like doing is watching TV.

Mom says the docter will know what to do in a few days. I hope You help him figger it out fast.

Your frend,
Luke

Something to Think About: The Diagnosis

Shaking off the effects of the lingering anesthesia, I willed my eyelids to open. Faces around my bedside gradually came into focus. Concerned faces. I looked for the white coat: the garment of authority, of knowledge, of salvation.

The white coat held my hand. I knew before a single word cut through the silence, but I asked anyway. "Is it cancer?"

"I'm afraid so." The white coat squeezed my fingers.

"What kind?"

Silence shouted the answer from the walls before the white coat spoke. "Invasive."

"How big?"

"Big enough."

More silence.

I could hear everyone not breathing. I retreated behind my closed eyes. I needed to think clearly. Information must be gathered. Decisions must be made.

"Later," I muttered as I allowed the blackness of drugged sleep to embrace me. "I will think later."

The miracle of changing water into wine at the wedding in Cana, as recorded in the Gospel of John, chapter two, marked the beginning of Jesus' earthly ministry. Did He realize His journey had begun? Did His mind fill with the enormity of what lay ahead? Did He have thoughts of going back to heaven and talking over the plan with God? When the wedding guests had gone home that night and when He closed His eyes in sleep, perhaps He consoled Himself by thinking, *Later. I'll think about it later.*

Just as I knew the diagnosis before a word was spoken, so Jesus knew. I knew my journey would be solitary, yet crowded with people; so Jesus knew. As I knew my courage would be tested to its limits, so Jesus knew.

But I also knew God would not desert me. Jesus knew that too. Though the diagnosis was devastating, it could never be an acceptable reason to curl up and die. There was work to do, healing to be sought. Whether the healing would be earthly or heavenly did not matter. What mattered was the work He would accomplish through me. I had to stay centered on Him. It was a job for which I did not apply, but nonetheless had been given.

Within the initial cyclone of spinning emotions and the turmoil of uncertainty, the greatest gift anyone can give is allowing time for withdrawal. Peace is sweet when God stretches His hand into the cyclone, holds your heart, and says, "It's okay. I've got hold of you."

CHAPTER TWO

Council with the Munchkins

When Dorothy woke up from her nap she saw some strange little people coming toward her. They called themselves Munchkins. With them was the Good Witch of the North, who thanked Dorothy for killing the Wicked Witch of the East and for freeing the Munchkin people from their bondage to her. Dorothy had no idea how this had happened.

She felt overcome with homesickness for Kansas. The Good Witch told Dorothy to follow the yellow brick road to Oz, where the Great Wizard would surely know how to help her go home. The journey ahead would sometimes be pleasant and sometimes dark and terrible.

Whether waiting for arrival or departure, all journeys begin by sitting still. For it is in the waiting that God gives appetite for the journey.

Stay with God! Take heart. Don't quit. I'll say it again: Stay with God.
—Psalm 27:14

Louis writes…

Okay, Lord,

Guess I have to face it—I hardly know You. And I hardly know my two boys and daughter. But I think I know Jan.

Last year was our fiftieth anniversary. Kids had a big wingding for us. People I hadn't seen for years came out of the woodwork to help us celebrate. I don't expect I'll see any of them again. Folks don't usually like to come around when you're this sick.

Deep down I think they're afraid of catching it. They never know what to say, so they don't want to sit down or stay very long. They talk about the weather or the last big storm, then make some excuse and leave.

Except Jan. We've been through a few things, her and me. We can talk about anything. She doesn't back away from any subject.

Like the year I turned fifty. Got it in my head that I didn't want to be married anymore. I told Jan I'd had enough and wanted to leave. She said, "Really? Seems like you should have thought about that thirty years ago when you married me. It's too late to be leaving me now." Then she looked me in the eye, kissed me hard on the mouth, smiled, and went off to buy some groceries for dinner. So I stayed.

Seems stupid now. But we do some things along the way that we're not proud of.

Like with Danny, my oldest boy. Lord, I'm going to need Your help smoothing things over with that boy. I blew it with him when he turned eighteen. I wanted him doing more than pumping gas for a living. He was bound and determined to get out on his own, to make his own way. I can't fault him for that. But I sure did want him to go to college.

He was smart enough. Never saw a twelve-year-old kid take apart a lawn mower engine and put it back together again like he did. Loved doing it too.

Last time I saw him, he was storming out of the house. Face was beet red. Hollering at me to beat the band. Of course, I did my share of hollering too. I told him not to come home unless he'd signed up for classes down at the community college.

He said he was old enough to run his own life and that I'd better not be telling him what to do. I told him I wanted my son to be more than a grease monkey. He looked like he'd been punched in the stomach. Probably should have kept that to myself.

He didn't come home again—not while I was around anyway. I think Jan must have gathered up his clothes and stuff. I bet he came to collect them when I was at work. Be darned if he didn't save enough from his gas station job to move to California. He calls and talks to his mother every now and then. She fills me in some.

Guess he's doing all right. Went to mechanic's school, runs his own shop. He even found a nice girl to marry. They have two kids…both girls. Never seen the wife or the daughters, only pictures.

I know it hurts Jan to have grandkids she hasn't seen, but she doesn't say anything about it.

Like I said, Lord, I've done some things I'm not proud of. It's probably time to swallow some humble pie, tell Danny I'm sorry, and ask him to come home.

Doc's going to run another test on me next week before they start the chemo. I haven't figured out exactly what the test is for but Doc says it's got to be done.

Sure would feel good to see Danny before I get to looking all nasty. Wouldn't be bad to see the girls and the wife either. Never know how long I might have, and little girls should know their grandpa.

I know I don't deserve a break with Danny. But Lord, if You could see Your way clear to make this happen for me, I'd be real grateful. Thanks for all the other stuff You do for me too.

My prayer kind of rambles, and I'm sorry for that, but I'm sure You can make sense of it. Thanks again. And please help me with this Danny thing.
>Amen.

Trisha writes...

Dear God,

The waiting is killing me. I need to get this lump out of my body now! Are there really so many people waiting for surgery that I have to stand in line?

Two more weeks to go. It was bad enough waiting three weeks for the biopsy but since it's malignant, I naturally assumed the follow-up surgery would be immediate. Ha! Silly me.

After this is over, I'm going to submit a revision proposal to these health care providers, outlining improvements to make this system tolerable to the patient. Cost would be minimal but would greatly increase consumer satisfaction.

I'm talking about simple things. Like hanging pictures on the ceiling so people have something to look at while they're flat on their backs for forty minutes during a scan. Or offering a blanket for extra warmth. Dressing in a flimsy cotton gown and waiting in an air-conditioned room makes the patient feel like a popsicle in the freezer. And they should allow patients to choose what music to listen to during these lengthy procedures. Those minor adjustments would make the surroundings more personal and caring. This is not rocket science. Has nobody figured this out?

My nursing instructors taught me to put myself in the patients' shoes, to anticipate their needs and desires. But they didn't teach the art of waiting.

I can't concentrate enough to read the magazines in the waiting room. The televisions all have either news or idiotic talk shows. It all seems trivial and unimportant when weighed against the significance of the lump in my breast.

Forty-two years old and I may be facing the end of my life. The worst part is that I won't know if I'm near the end for two more weeks—until they can get in there and see the condition of my lymph nodes. Two more weeks of waiting and watching life happen around me. Two more weeks of seeing my husband's eyes carefully gauge my every expression, trying to determine my mood. Two more weeks of wondering if Troy will still desire me physically after this is all over.

God, only You know what's going through his mind. He's been measuring every word he says to me. He's probably afraid I'll fall apart and cry. He hates it when I cry. I wish he'd just come right out and get mad that I'm having to go through this.

Steven is only twelve years old and I'm still reading stories to him each night before bed. It's our special time together when he can kick back and not have to be a "cool" middle-schooler. He's a bright kid. He's the son of a nurse, after all. He knew what the word *diarrhea* meant when he was three.

And he knows what cancer means. When I told him about the lump, he simply asked how the doctor would treat it. I told him about the surgery and the possibility of chemotherapy and losing my hair, and he said he'd share his baseball cap collection with me if I wanted to wear some of them.

I swallowed a big lump in my throat right then and my eyes filled with hot tears. I had to turn away for a minute to pull myself together.

Lord, You know how much I love that boy. I can't imagine leaving him to go through high school without me. I know Troy would do a good job but sometimes a guy needs a mom to hug.

I don't want to leave him. I don't want to leave Troy. I don't want to leave this earth. And I don't want to wait.

Two...more...weeks. It may as well be a lifetime. I hope I won't have to pay for the wait with my life. All it takes is a couple of aggressive cells making their way out into the lymph system. These doctors know this but they still make me wait.

I hate this, Lord God. And I'm still not sure how I feel about You right now.

So again, I won't say amen because I'm still not finished with You yet.

Luke writes...

Dear Jesus,
   It isn't werking.
   The docter put another needle in my arm and took more of my blood. I'm still tired. This morning, rite after I woke up, I was breething hard. Like I had run down and back the whole soccer field without stopping.
   Mom called the docter. I went back to bed. She propped me up on a pillo and laid beside me, and she sang the songs she used to sing to me when I was a baby. I don't remember that, but that's what she said.
   It was kinda nice. I closed my eyes and lissened to her, and I forgot I was breething hard. And then I felt a little better.
   But I'm still tired. So pleese tell the docter to try something else. I think he needs Your help. Could You pleese tell him something to try without a needle? And to do it soon? I'm tired of being tired.
             Thank You very much.
             Your frend,
             Luke

Something to Think About: Waiting

Fourteen more days and my breast would be gone. Fourteen days to say farewell to a body part I had grown to love. I slipped my hand under my shirt, reaching for the familiar softness.

Not too long ago, the tiny fumbling fingers of my baby groped for the nourishment my breast offered. I slid my thumb lightly over the center area and experienced a faint tingle. I supposed sensations would be gone too. I worried about my husband's reactions to the coming vacancy.

Fourteen days. Was it enough time to permanently imprint all the memories on my mind and heart? I wanted to remember everything.

I smiled slightly as I recalled the anxious girlhood years of waiting for the flatness to go away. I remembered when Mom and I made a trip to the store to buy an expandable bra with a tag that read, "Perfect for training young, growing figures." I recalled the first time I walked out of the house wearing it, wondering if people could see a difference.

I wondered the same thing now. Would people be able to see which side of my chest was not real? Abruptly, I pulled my hand away.

What did it matter?

It matters.

Mark tells about a Sabbath morning when Jesus went to church and saw a man with a shriveled hand (Mark 3:1–6). Jesus told the man to "stand up in front of everyone" (NIV).

Ouch.

The church seemed full of eyes, all focused on the useless body part, something the man had probably spent most of his life trying to hide. But he stood because Jesus asked him to stand. Jesus was about to give him much more than restored function of his hand.

With the words "Stand up in front of everyone," Jesus showed His mastery over every situation. He used affliction to draw others to Himself.

As the time for separation from my body part grew closer and my frustration with waiting grew more intense, I read this account in Mark many times. I was reminded that my entire body was a gift from God and that He has a right to use it any way He chooses. I knew God did not point a finger from heaven and say, "Strike her with cancer." I also knew He could use the cancer to bring others closer to knowing Him.

I was simply the vehicle for making it happen.

I wondered how God would use a lopsided chest. I just had to wait and see. This meant waiting with grace. Waiting with patience. Waiting with humility.

And most of all, waiting with faith. Giving Him credit for life is paramount.

It's often difficult for us to comprehend how precious life is until we are threatened by its loss. Waiting is a gift. Whether the wait is for test results or for a turn at the drive-through bank, waiting brings time for reflection and thankfulness. It's essential to give a hurting heart time to grieve, and it's important to realize that sighing and crying are part of the process.

There are no magical words to make it hurt less.

Experiencing pain means the heart is full of life. When family members and friends refrain from spouting empty reassurances, but stand alongside you through the wait, the journey seems not only palatable, but uplifting.

CHAPTER THREE

How Dorothy Saved the Scarecrow

Dorothy set off on her journey to find the Wizard of Oz, believing he could tell her how to get home to Kansas. Along the way she encountered a scarecrow stuck on a pole in a cornfield. The scarecrow asked her to take away the pole, and when she complied, he thanked her. When he found out she was going to Oz, he decided to go along and ask the wizard for some brains.

Scarecrow told Dorothy he could not be injured because his arms and legs were filled with straw and that his deepest wish was that people would not think of him as a fool. Thus, his request for brains from the wizard. He also told Dorothy he would carry the basket for her because he never got tired. There was only one thing Scarecrow truly feared…a lighted match.

Receiving a ticket to ride in God's hot-air balloon is a gift of immense proportions. Being lifted above the ordinary can be somewhat dizzying, but eventually, it will clear the cloudiest of muddled thinking.

> You're my cave to hide in, my cliff to climb. Be my safe leader, be my true mountain guide. Free me from hidden traps; I want to hide in you.
>
> —Psalm 31:3–4

Louis writes…

>   Dear Lord,
>   I should have come to You years ago. You really do seem to hear most of what I say. The kids are coming around, except for Danny. He may be a lost cause, even for You.
>   Michael and his bunch came by this morning and JoEllen stopped in this afternoon. I guess they all wanted to get a good look at me before I start this chemo thing on Monday.
>   JoEllen wanted to know if I planned on going to church services tomorrow. I wonder if Doc has told Jan and the kids more than he's told me. Must be really serious if JoEllen's asking me about church. She's never been very religious. Always has marched to her own drummer. I just wish she'd find some guy and get married. Doesn't seem natural for a woman to live by herself—no husband or kids. Can't imagine she could be very happy.
>   JoEllen's got herself a good job though. And she's got gumption. I have to give her credit for that. She's been working herself up the ladder at the bank, giving those guys a run for their money.
>   She always did like money. I remember coming across her little stash of birthday and allowance cash when she was about eleven. She had stuffed it into the toe of a fuzzy black sock. I said, "JoEllen, what do you plan on doing with all that money?" She looked up at me with those big, serious blue eyes and said, "Well, Daddy, I'm just going to keep it for a while. I may need to use it for something I haven't even thought of yet."
>   Yes, that girl likes to be ready for anything. But going to church? I wonder if she goes. Never asked her. Maybe I should.
>   I guess I don't know my kids anymore. I wonder when that happened. Jan's always been the one to stay close…but then, she's their mother. Mothers know what kids need. It's

the mother's job to raise them up right. My job was making sure she had the means to do it.

It was rough doing my job during their high school years. I think it was probably around that time when I lost touch with them. There was always some crisis or another going on around the house. Homework, projects, school dances, kids running in and out at all hours. I couldn't stand the commotion. We nearly went broke trying to keep food on the table. But Jan was amazing at making the money stretch. And she did a good job with the kids, all things considered.

I remember only one time I had to intervene. Michael and his blasted speeding tickets. Jan has a soft spot for Michael. She won't admit it, but he's her favorite child. Sometimes I think she loves him more than me. He looks a lot like her.

Michael got himself into a fix with the law one night. It was nearly midnight and I'd been sleeping hard for a couple of hours. I woke up for some reason and saw Jan wasn't in bed. I didn't think too much of it since she sometimes stays up late reading.

Anyway, I went to the kitchen to get some water and saw the front porch light was on. When I walked over to turn it off, I saw some people standing on my doorstep. Made my heart turn over in my chest. It was Michael, Jan, and a police officer. Michael had been pulled over for "excessive speeding," but instead of giving him a ticket, the officer brought him home to face us.

Michael's face was wet from crying and Jan looked like she'd been hit in the gut. The officer was shorter and looked younger than Michael, but he was reading him the riot act loud and clear. Told Michael it was a merciful act of God that he was still alive and breathing. I guess he'd been doing eighty or so through the center of town and could have jumped a curb and hit a tree or pole, or worse yet, a pedestrian or another car with someone in it.

Come to find out, Michael had had two other speeding tickets. Jan knew about them and had worked out a payment plan for him, and he had sworn to her he'd never go over the speed limit again.

She held out her hand to the officer, asked for Michael's license, and said Michael wouldn't be using it again for a very long time. The officer must have believed her because he handed it over, shook his head, and said, "If there ever is a next time, the cost may be more than you can bear."

Then he turned and walked off to his patrol car. And Michael watched his mother crumple in front of his eyes.

I'd seen Jan upset before, but not like this. I think it hit her hard that she could have lost her boy. She was heaving and sobbing and kept saying, "You could have been killed. You could have been killed."

Michael wrapped her in his arms, and he was crying, too, saying, "I'm sorry, I'm sorry," over and over.

I'm no good with all this emotional stuff. Just watching them made my eyes brim over. So when Michael came inside, I just glared at him and said, "Three months. No car for three months." Then I went to bed. Don't know how long they stayed up…must have been most of the night, judging from how they looked the next day.

Those two are still pretty tight. Guess spending nights like that one will do it to you. Almost wish I could have stuck it out, let myself go, and cried with them. But it's no use. I am who I am. Doubt that will ever change.

Maybe I do need to go to church tomorrow. I have no idea what this chemo will bring. It may knock the daylights out of this disease, or it might just knock the stuffing out of me and leave the cancer to eat me up.

Something big must be coming down the pike, Lord. You've let my mind wander all over the place. Haven't reminisced this much in a long time. I think I'm going to need Your help more than I realized.

Sorry it's taken me so long to figure that out.

I think I'll ask Jan to call JoEllen. We should all go to church together.

So…I guess that's it then.
Amen.

Trisha writes…

Lord,

In case You're at all interested in what's been happening to me, my breast is gone now. They took it all. Down to the bone. Soft tissue, muscle, a few lymph nodes. All of it.

The nodes had some cancerous cells. Dr. Leverman was somewhat vague about the extent. But I have to admit, he has been extremely caring and helpful in giving me options.

I have read everything I could find on the subject, but even with knowing the language, it's been difficult to weigh all the possibilities. Right now, it sounds as if a full course of chemotherapy and radiation would be the best way to go.

I'm tempted to take the natural route because it's quite effective in boosting the immune system. But I'm not convinced it would do the job on whatever may be left floating around in my body.

I wish Troy would offer his opinion on it. He keeps saying, "You're the nurse; you know best." True. I am the nurse. I almost wish I wasn't. I know what's ahead and it's not going to be pleasant. Even if things go smoothly, it won't be an easy ride.

It seems as if everyone expects me to handle this better because I am a nurse. What a joke. Do they think my stomach doesn't turn over at the thought of a long, drawn-out battle in which I either waste away to skin and bones or puff up like a blowfish from all the steroids? Do they think I lay my head on my pillow each night and blissfully fall asleep without wondering how many more nights I have to live? Do they really think being a nurse makes me immune from *feeling*?

Since the surgery, I've followed my doctor's instructions to the letter. I've forged ahead with the exercises, meticulously measured output from the drain tubes, and changed dressings using my best sterile technique.

I've done at least a thousand dressing changes on other people, but doing it on myself is quite a trick. It's difficult to do with one hand. Troy helped me at first, but I could see by the sudden lack of color in his face that I was asking for a bit more than he could give. No matter…it's enough to know he loves me. And I'm thankful he's handling Steven's needs. Meals, laundry, all the house stuff.

Steven's turned out to be a real treasure. It doesn't seem to bother him in the least to empty my drain tubes. I don't think many kids his age could handle it. And instead of me tucking him into bed every night, he is now doing it for me. He snuggles beside me on top of the covers and we talk about his day and even a little about my day. When we're finished, he leans over, kisses me on the forehead, and says, "Sleep good, Mom. Say your prayers. I'll see you in the morning." It's the same thing I've told him every night for the past twelve years.

I wonder if he's giving me the whole story of his days or if he's leaving out the parts that might upset me. I also wonder what he will grow up to be. I hope I'm around to see him go to college, find a girl, marry, and have children. My grandchildren.

Surely You will allow me these simple pleasures of life, won't You, Lord? It's almost time for an old-fashioned, spill-my-guts, heart-to-heart talk with You. I'd do it today, but I need to save my energy for the coming week. It's going to be a tough one—getting the drains removed and preparing for the first round of chemo. I realize You have my best interests in mind and truly do love me, but it's hard to figure out why You're allowing all this to happen.

Stay close, will You, Father? I've got this big empty place on my chest now. I don't want another big empty place in my heart.

I'll be talking to You again.

Amen. I guess.

Luke writes…

Dear Jesus,

Thanks for making Mom happy again. She hasn't been smiling much since I got sick. But she talked to the doctor a long time today after he looked at me and he said he was going to do something to make me better.

I was happy to hear the news too. Except Mom says it will be another needle thing. The needle will have medisin to make me sleep, and when I'm sleeping, the docter will put a tube in my chest. I will wake up and then he will put more medisin in the tube, so it will go inside me and fix whatever is making me so tired.

I hope it werks. I'm afraid the guys will get that new kid named Curtis to play on the teem instead of me and I'll never get my spot back. Curtis is all right and everything, but he doesn't know much about soccer. He told me they didn't have soccer where he lived before. Only baseball. The guys will need to get somebody if I can't do it and I know they'd take Curtis before they'd take one of the girls.

I just have to get better. It would be great if You would help the docter with the tube and everything. It's a pretty new invention, I guess, so You might have to read up on it before You try to help. But I bet You're pretty smart since You made the world and everything.

I think that's all for now.

               Your friend,
               Luke

P.S. I hope things are going good for You up there in heven.

Something to Think About: Fast Forward

I looked into the fresh, eager face of my teenage son. He perched on the edge of my bed as he gave a lengthy dissertation of the day's events. With my ears, I listened to him speak about school and friends and the new friend he'd met in math class. With my heart, I saw him in a groom's tuxedo as he might appear a few short years from now.

I wasn't sure I had a few short years. I believed in God. I trusted in the Lord's ability to do miracles and to heal terminal illnesses—even mine. I prayed continually for personal healing. But for some reason, God wasn't giving me a definite answer yet.

So I used the time He gave me to push the fast-forward button in my mind. Thanking God for the gift of imagination, I saw my young son in a black and white tuxedo, standing in the front of a church, ready to receive his bride.

My place in the pew was empty.

The organ began the wedding march. I saw him look at the empty seat. He smiled slightly and placed his hand over his heart. He missed me.

Then he saw his bride standing at the back of the church, ready to make the life-changing walk. His slight smile transformed into a wide grin as their eyes met.

He was ready. She was radiant. They would be fine.

I had given him my best and it would be enough.

Learning to hunger for heaven takes time. During the learning process, the pull of life on earth is strong. When we are presented with an uncertain future, it is normal to spend time thinking about what we may miss in the future. In spite of the promises of a care-free, pain-free existence in heaven, our human nature clings to the known elements of earth.

This doesn't mean we don't want to go to heaven. It simply means we've enjoyed our time on earth. Nothing is wrong with that. God gave us the earth to enjoy. He is aware of the conflicting emotions we experience during this transition.

As we contemplate life in heaven, we also think about what life will be like for our family after we die. We long to see our sons and daughters graduate from high school and college, marry, and have children. We have waves of remorse and sadness when we realize there is a possibility we won't see this happen. And we don't even want to think about a time when our spouses might remarry.

But this doesn't mean our faith is not strong or that we are dragging our feet on the way to heaven. Heaven offers much more than earth ever could. Most of us can remember closing our eyes and whispering, "Take me now, Lord. Take me now." The debilitating nature of pain has a way of increasing our longing for a final, lasting peace and freedom.

During dark hours of severe illness, withdrawing deep into oneself is both protective and restorative. While we linger in the darkness, God reaches through the murky haze and whispers to our suffering hearts, "I am even here."

Nothing brings as much hope and comfort as His voice. Isaiah says, "O Master, these are the conditions in which people live, and yes, in these very conditions my spirit is still alive—fully recovered with a fresh infusion of life! It seems it was good for me to go through all those troubles. Throughout them all you held tight to my lifeline. You never let me tumble over the edge into nothing. (Isaiah 38:16–17)

CHAPTER FOUR

The Road Through the Forest

Dorothy, her dog Toto, and the scarecrow followed the yellow brick road. Dorothy told Scarecrow about how gray Kansas was, and he asked why she would want to return there. Her answer came quickly: There's no place like home.

The yellow brick road led into a thick forest, where trees obstructed the daylight. The two travelers bravely forged ahead. They came upon a cottage, where Dorothy and Toto stopped to rest for the night while the scarecrow stood in a corner of the cottage to wait patiently until morning.

Thorns may inflict pain before you smell the blooming rose. It all depends on where you hold the stem.

> I know what I'm doing. I have it all planned out—plans to take care of you, not abandon you, plans to give you the future you hope for.
>
> —Jeremiah 29:11

Louis writes…

Lord,

This is way more than I want to handle. I suppose it's gotta be done, but I've never liked doctors. They think they

41

know everything or at least they try to convince me that they do. Makes me feel like I'm less of a man. Like I can't handle my own life.

Maybe it's true. I sure can't handle this part of it. I want to rip this needle out of my arm, walk out the door, and never look back. I guess I'm stuck because I don't think it's my time to go yet. They just need to fix me up so I can get on about my business of being retired.

Can't stand the smell of this clinic. It's too clean or something. Sort of like the kitchen floor after Jan mops it. Can't believe I have to stay here all day breathing it in. I figured I'd show up, they'd put in the intravenous, it'd take about an hour, and then I'd be done.

Didn't work out like I thought at all. First they took some of my blood. The nurse tried to make a joke out of it…said it was like "before and after" pictures of my blood. She's coming back with an intravenous so I won't get sick to my stomach during the chemo. Then they'll give me another IV for something else I can't remember and run that through. Finally we get to the treatment. I bet they give me some more intravenous after that. With all the liquid going through me, I guess I know where I'll be spending my time today.

At least they've got a decent recliner for me to sit in. The footrest goes up on it. Not bad for a doctor's office. The nurse gave me a blanket and pillow. Surely she doesn't think I'll sleep through this.

Oh boy…here we go. She's ready to hook me up. Lord, give me strength. And as long as You're here, it'd be good if You would go ahead and heal me. Might save You a trip later—not that I don't want to have You come around again.

I did go to church yesterday. I bet You did a double-take when I walked in the door. Jan and JoEllen seemed pleased I went along with them. I'll have to do some more thinking on this church thing.

The Road Through the Forest

Whoa! They're making those needles bigger every day. I sure felt that one go in. Good thing Jan will be driving home. My arm's going to be sore.

Here it comes. The anti-throw-up medicine. It's dripping in pretty fast. Shouldn't take long at this rate. Good deal. Like I always told the kids, "If you have to do something difficult, dig in your heels and get it over with quick."

Hey, this doesn't seem like bad stuff. Mouth is kind of dry, though. I think it's flushing the spit right out of me. I wonder if I should tell somebody about my head. It kind of feels woozy, like I had a few too many beers.

Then again, if this is as bad as it gets, I can handle it. I think I'll take advantage of this pillow and close my eyes awhile.

I wonder if Jan called Danny yet...

Trisha writes...

Well, Lord, one step is behind me, with another flight of stairs to conquer before this is finished. Drains are out; incisions are healing. Now the fun begins. Portacath insertion is tomorrow.

At least I didn't have to convince Dr. Leverman of its merits. He already knew. I've watched too many people being tortured as nurses and lab techs try to insert catheters into overused veins. Thank goodness this doctor seems to be on top of the latest developments.

With the portacath insertion, I won't have to be stuck ninety times before they can run the chemo into my circulatory system. One needle stick through a rubber stopper planted under my skin, and they're in.

Guess it's time to think about the hair situation. I'm going to have to do something this week because I know I won't have a lot of energy to deal with it later. My options: (1) Cut it real short now and shave it as it all starts to fall out and then buy a wig. (2) Shave it all now, buy the wig, and be done with it. (3) Ignore the whole thing, buy a wig just for fun, and wear it when my head starts to look as if I caught a skin disease from a dog. Or I could wear Steven's baseball caps and forget the wig entirely.

I wish Troy would tell me what he's thinking. He's never been around anybody with cancer. Maybe that's a good thing. Lord, I pray that You will keep us together through this. There are so many directions this road could take...and none of them are going to be easy.

Maybe when they put me to sleep tomorrow for the portacath, You'll let me sleep forever. What a smooth, simple way to leave this world. I wouldn't have this hair thing to decide. I wouldn't wonder if Troy will still love me when I look like a concentration camp victim. And then I would finally find out how wonderful heaven is.

I do love You, Lord. You've known that since the beginning. I'm just a little mad about having to do this because it wasn't in my plan. I haven't yet figured out why it's in Your plan for me. Seems to me I could do more for You if I were strong and healthy.

But what do I know? I don't have Your insight, I don't have Your vision, I don't have Your wisdom. But I do have You. And that's the important thing.

When I'm by myself, I like to curl up in my cushy, oyster-colored recliner and wrap myself in the afghan Aunt Gen crocheted for me. I feel so close to You then. I know as surely as I breathe that You are with me. I feel Your arms holding me secure in the afghan. I lean my head against Your shoulders. I hear Your voice telling my heart everything's going to turn out fine.

And everything will. One way or another.

Lord God, countless times I've heard the story of what You did for me on the cross of Calvary. Countless times I've thanked You for what you did. And countless times I've walked away giving it no more thought than a weather report. I am only now beginning to grasp a tiny sliver of awareness of what it cost You for the greatest act of love mankind has ever known.

Thank You for that awareness. Thanks for letting me count on You. No matter what happens tomorrow, I know You have it handled.

Because I am still Your child. Your Trisha.

Amen.

Luke writes...

Hi, Jesus.

How are You? I am fine. Sort of. The tube is in my chest. The medisin will go in tomorrow. I asked the docter how long before I get well. He said maybe by chrismas. That's a long time away. It's not even summer outside.

I thought the medisin would go in and I would be okay right after. But I'm not. Should I tell Mom? She'll probly get mad. She might even cry.

I guess Curtis will take my place on the teem. That makes me mad. But I won't cry. If I don't cry, maybe Mommy won't either.

Will You plese make the medisin work tomorrow? Then maybe we won't have to tell Mom about the chrismas thing.

Your frend,
Luke

Something to Think About: Instant Access

"You want to put a porta-what in me?"

"A portacath. A catheter implanted under your skin," the surgeon patiently explained. "We will have instant access to your veins for chemotherapy. It will save you from the discomfort of searching for good veins. It will only require one needle stick each time you come."

"And that's a good thing?" I asked.

"That is a real good thing. Believe me."

"I guess I have to." I took a deep breath and picked up the pen to sign the surgery permission form.

Who would have thought anyone would need instant access to my veins?

Three months later, I watched a nurse strain to insert a catheter into the overused vein of a fellow chemotherapy patient. I tried not to stare at the big round bump under her right collarbone. After several attempts, the nurse finally slid the catheter into place and everyone in the room breathed a collective sigh of relief. Access had been achieved. The treatment could continue.

I never imagined I would feel such thankfulness for this ugly, hard object under my skin. The surgeon had told the truth. Instant access was a good thing.

Jesus vividly explained the beauty of instant access in the Gospel of John. "It's urgent that you listen carefully to this: Anyone here who believes what I am saying right now and aligns himself with the Father, who has in fact put me in charge, has at this very moment the real, lasting life and is no longer condemned to be an outsider. This person has taken a giant step from the world of the dead to the world of the living" (John 5:24).

Instant access to heaven is gained through simple belief in the truth. Jesus opened heaven's doors for us by enduring the needle sticks of thorns on His head, a sword in His side, and nails in His hands and feet.

Jesus is our Portacath, our instant access into heaven.

Hear it. Believe it. Live forever.

No more needle sticks.

CHAPTER FIVE

The Rescue of the Tin Woodman

Dorothy, Toto, and the scarecrow left the cottage and walked to a spring, where they found water for drinking and bathing. There they discovered a man entirely made of tin who seemed to be frozen, unable to move his joints. Dorothy rescued him by oiling his joints with a nearby oilcan. As she worked, the tin woodsman told them of his desire for a heart. He decided to join them on their journey to Oz, where he could ask the wizard to grant his wish.

Dorothy wondered if her new friends would be granted their requests. She also worried that she did not have enough food to live on.

Heavenly food always seems hardest to chew and swallow. But it nurtures both the body and the soul rather than one or the other.

> God spoke to Moses, "I've listened to the complaints of the Israelites. Now tell them: 'At dusk you will eat meat and at dawn you'll eat your fill of bread; and you'll realize that I am God, your God.'"
>
> —Exodus 16:11–12

Louis writes…

Lord,

I thought I'd be finished with this treatment by now. I wonder when all these other people got here. Looks like they're all hooked up to the intravenous too. I must have slept through everything.

Here comes the nurse with a new bag. Oh, great. It's for me. Surely this has to be the last one. I feel as if I've been here a hundred years. But at least I don't have to be stuck again.

Were You surprised to see me in church yesterday, Lord? It wasn't too bad, all things considered. People seemed nice. Felt sort of good to be there. I only knew one song though—"How Great Thou Art," the one George Beverly Shea sings on television at Billy Graham crusades.

Funny how good a song can make you feel. Here I am thinking about dying and leaving Jan and the kids, and I could still sing about nature and trees and how great You are. Maybe I'll tell Jan to have it sung at my funeral, which is not going to be anytime soon if I have anything to say about it.

I can't believe You gave me this awful disease. Nobody is mean enough to wish this on anyone, but especially not You. I know I don't have the best track record on churchgoing, but it doesn't make sense that You would make people suffer on purpose. And I know there's worse suffering to come.

I wonder what would have happened if I'd just kept doctoring myself with a little more Vicks cough syrup. Nobody would have known the tumor was there. Maybe it would have gone away.

Isn't this bag of intravenous ever going to run out? It seems as if it's dripping too slow.

I'm going nuts with all these people around me acting like this is a big social gathering. They keep trying to talk to me, but I'm not here to make friends. I just want to get this over with. Besides, I've got my own problems to think about..

Check out the guy with the ball cap over there, playing poker with the farmer in overalls. I wonder if they're betting whose intravenous is going to finish first or who is going to live the longest? Morbid. This whole thing is so odd.

I've never in my life spent so much time wondering what other people are thinking. Must be the drugs.

The guy with the ball cap has an intravenous going in somewhere up by his shoulder. I wonder why. He must have a bad case. He probably doesn't have any hair under that ball cap. Sure hope I keep my hair awhile yet.

What's going on? It feels like my groin's on fire! I wonder if I need to tell somebody about this. Hold on, Lord, while I try to get the nurse's attention.

What a relief! She said the "hot groin" is a side effect of one of the drugs. And hot really means *hot!* No kidding, it felt like my shorts had come out of the oven. Sure hope I don't have to go through that again.

A few more drips through the tube and I'm out of here. With any luck, I can doze off again and wake up when it's finished. Of course that won't happen if these people don't keep the noise down. Can't believe they're laughing and joking around. I wonder what they think about when they go to bed at night.

I can't believe I have to come back and sit here again tomorrow and the next day.

Guess I'll be talking to you more later, Lord.
      Amen.

Trisha writes...

 This portacath is going to be the thorn in my flesh (or shoulder, actually) for the next six months. It didn't look this big when I saw it before the surgery. My skin is stretched tight across the top of it. It looks like the top of a miniature drum imbedded under my clavicle. It feels like I've got one of Steven's Legos under my skin.

I have to be careful moving either arm because I don't want to mess up anything or tear out the sutures. Of course the doctor had to put it exactly where my bra strap goes. I'm sure he didn't give a thought to the inconvenience of the location. I guess I won't be going anywhere too nice for a while. I'm not brave enough to be in public without proper support. I haven't bought a prosthesis yet anyway, since the incision's too raw.

I'm thankful we have good insurance with my job. My supervisor didn't think twice about letting me use up my sick leave. She said we'd talk if I needed more once it was gone.

It's been a tiring day. I sat in my "thinking chair" this afternoon, closed my eyes, and tried to curl up in a little ball. I wish I could push Rewind and make all this not happen, or push Fast Forward and have it all be finished. I long for my body to be comfortable in its skin again, although I know it won't happen for a long, long time.

Lord, You've brought me to the beginning of another chapter in my life. Tomorrow I begin chemotherapy. I'd rather not have to endure it, but at least I can take comfort in the fact that all chapters have an ending. One way or another, Your plan will be carried through. Right now, I can think of nothing except keeping some sense of normalcy in the house for Troy and Steven. I'm not sure it's possible.

The nurse at the clinic said I could come anytime beginning at eight in the morning. The treatment all needs to be finished by seven o'clock in the evening, so the last beginning infusion time would be around two in the afternoon. I'd like to get it finished as quickly as possible so I still have some time left to pull myself together before Steven gets home from school and Troy gets home from work. Guess I'll try to be at the clinic early.

Marcy from church offered to drive me to my treatments. Most likely I'll only experience some slight fatigue afterward. The nurse said I could probably drive myself.

But I don't want to chance it. I don't want to go through the frustration of trying to find a place to park in that crowded garage anyway. Marcy used to work in the area of the clinic so she's comfortable with the traffic and congestion. I'm very thankful she agreed to take me.

I'm a little uneasy about my prognosis. The doctor said he *thinks* he got all the cancer when he took out my breast and a few lymph nodes. Unfortunately, two of the nodes were affected. Both the surgeon and the oncologist said they believed a couple of rounds of chemo were best for insurance purposes and that would "do the trick." Easy for them to say. They can go home to their healthy, energetic lives and be normal.

Dear Lord, I want so much for this treatment to be effective. I don't want to do more than one round. I've seen what happens to people who go through this. I'm ashamed to say I've never asked them what they were thinking or feeling as they endured it. I guess it's more comfortable to concentrate on the physical symptoms instead. Physical things seem easier to fix.

Thank You for my church family, Lord. At service last Sunday, the pastor announced that a special prayer time for me would be held right after the service. A lot of people stayed. I didn't even know some of them. As I sat in that little room and looked at the faces, I saw my some of my feelings mirrored in their eyes. Concern, hope, faith in Your plan, and of course, some fear.

We formed a circle—like kids getting ready to play Duck, Duck, Goose at recess. But instead of a child running around the outside of the circle, the presence of the Holy Spirit blanketed our hearts. Instead of taking turns being "it," they took turns praying for me.

Our hands were joined, and the support felt tangible. My nose ran and quiet tears dripped down my cheeks and soaked my blouse, but I didn't let go of their hands. I wanted to take the whole circle home with me. If it were possible, I'd bring them all with me to my first treatment.

When they finished praying, I got the feeling they didn't wanted to let go either. One by one, they came up to me. Some wished me well. Some prayed again. Some kissed me. Some cried. Everyone hugged me. Everyone promised more prayers. Never have I experienced such an intense, emotional outpouring of love and support from so many people at one time. I knew in my heart everything would turn out exactly the way You want it to.

I'm still a bit uneasy about tomorrow, but the fear is gone.

For any one of those people from church, those men and women equipped with such giant-size loving and serving hearts, I'd happily walk to China and back. So I guess I can ride downtown with Marcy tomorrow and face those IV bags.

Thanks again, Lord, for getting the portacath into me without incident and for placing me in the middle of this devoted church family.

                Amen.

Luke's Mom writes...

Dear God,

I'm begging You...please let there be a place open for Luke in the chemo room tomorrow. I can't get away from work in time to take him across town to the pediatric unit. They'll fire me. If I lose my job, I lose the insurance, and I'll have no way to take care of Luke's illness. God in heaven, hear me tonight. Make that phone ring!

My baby needs that chemo. I know I messed up when I got pregnant, but that's not Luke's fault. Please, please, please, hear me! These past seven years have been the best of my life because of him. We're trying hard to do everything right. So please let a spot open up for him. I know it means he has to be with adults, but Luke is different from most kids. He won't mind.

The Rescue of the Tin Woodman

Dear God, I don't ask You for much. I'm begging You to make this happen for us. Luke can't afford to wait much longer for therapy. You know what's in our future. We really need a head start on this.

I don't know what else to say. I've cried all I can cry. My throat is tight and dry. I've filled out every form known to every health care system. My hand is cramped.

I've told Luke I will take care of him no matter what. But my heart is so heavy.

I give up, Lord. I've done all I can do. It's in Your hands. I guess it always was. Please give my little boy a chance to be well again. He's just a child. Let him have a life!

Your will be done. And Your will better let Luke live.
      Amen.

Luke writes...

Dear Jesus,

Mommy says I need some special medisin. She says if the phone rings we will go to the doctor tomorrow and I can forgit about school for a while. But if the phone doesn't ring I can sleep in. So whatever You think is best. I leeve it up to you. You are God.

I love You. I hope Your angels are being good. I'm going to sleep now.
      Your frend,
      Luke

Luke's Mom writes...

Lord God,

You really heard me, didn't You? Thank You for answering my prayer. I will have Luke ready first thing in the morning. Help him sleep soundly. Me too.

Please let there be people tomorrow who will take good care of him and watch out for him. I ache to stay with him but You know I can't. Anyway, thanks for making this happen. Let it go smoothly. He's such a little boy.
      Amen.

Something to Think About: Roads

The dry, smooth road mocked me. As the car glided easily over the surface of the freeway, I knew the closer I came to the exit leading to the medical center, the rougher the drive would become.

I looked out the windows of the car and pretended the road trip was my own choice. I noticed the buildings, trees, and signs. Nothing seemed to have changed since I made the journey yesterday.

Three exits to go. I pretended I was driving to Iowa…home. Smiling parents with open arms at the end of the trip—warm banana bread and steaming coffee. The memory dealt a soft blow to my stomach. My grip tightened around the steering wheel.

Two exits remaining. I wished I'd asked someone to come with me, just to provide a distraction. I could have picked up the phone and had company immediately. But sometimes, like today, the fight had to be fought alone. I needed to allow myself time to meander through the roads of my mind, to think about what I was facing, what I was enduring.

One exit left. Now I had to watch carefully I didn't want to fly past the turnoff. The exit was elevated: one narrow, curving lane going under an overpass. Raggedy people pushing grocery carts stacked with their belongings made their homes under the concrete shelter of the road. I fleetingly thought about stopping to visit with them, to ask them what they did when they became sick, to find out how they coped with the road on which they traveled.

I eased my foot from the accelerator, braking slightly to make the curve. The road grew uneven, with patches and potholes marring its surface. Yet I navigated successfully to the seven-story building with its attached parking garage.

I pulled up to the garage's entrance, pausing to take a ticket from the automated machine. Around and up, around and up, around and up I drove, finally stopping on the fourth level. I reached for my purse, removed the keys from the ignition, and paused. Leaning my head against the headrest, I closed my eyes, sighed, and said, "I wonder what the normal people are doing today."

CHAPTER SIX

The Cowardly Lion

Dorothy, the tin woodsman, and Toto made their way along the yellow brick road. As they traveled, they meet a cowardly lion, who decided to join them because he wanted to receive courage from the Wizard of Oz. The group welcomed him to their little company and resumed their journey together.

The unfolding bloom of courage discovered in illness flourishes when watered with hope, whether the hope is found in the breezes of heaven or in the winds of earth.

> In the same way I was with Moses, I'll be with you. I won't give up on you; I won't leave you. Strength! Courage! You are going to lead this people to inherit the land that I promised to give their ancestors. Give it everything you have, heart and soul.
> —Joshua 1:5–7

Louis writes…

> Lord Almighty,
> I thought I'd seen it all before today.
> When that little boy walked into the room, holding the nurse's hand, I felt like I'd had the breath knocked out of

me. Such a small boy. Big brown eyes, dark hair, red T-shirt, blue jeans. Strangely enough, he seemed more curious than afraid.

The nurse sat him down in the recliner closest to me—the one where the guy with the ball cap usually sits. She told me his name is Luke.

I tried to look away as they hooked the kid up to the IV bag. He has one of those gadgets under his skin by his shoulder. The nurse had to struggle with his T-shirt to get the bag hooked up underneath it. He tried hard to sit still while she was doing it, and he looked away from her. Probably was pretending he was somewhere else.

"Hi, Luke," I said, trying to help distract the boy. "My name's Louis."

"Hi," he said. His eyes were huge. His voice was tiny.

I wished I had something to give him, something to take his mind off of where he was and what was happening to him. But the best I could do was smile and close my eyes. I didn't want him to see I felt sorry for him.

At the end of the day I asked why the guy with the cap didn't show up. The nurse told me he passed away last evening. She seemed sad and said he had fought for a long time. I guess people in the medical profession have to get used to people dying.

I could never get used to little kids dying, though. I hope I don't have to watch Luke waste away.

Dear Lord, it's bad enough to put me and my family through this, but couldn't You leave the kid alone?

I wonder why nobody came with him. Doesn't seem right for the boy to go through something like this alone. He needs a family. Maybe You could see Your way clear to find one for him.

Speaking of families, Jan told me Danny finally answered her calls, so thanks for doing something about that situation. She said he didn't do much talking, mostly just listened. I guess he's going to try to swing a trip and come see us.

The Cowardly Lion

I wonder how she talked him into it after all these years. Gotta give her credit. She's good with words.

Michael's family and JoEllen are coming for the whole day on Saturday, and maybe Sunday too. Jan's wanting to do the picnic thing in the backyard. Probably should have done more of this through the years. Funny how looking at the end of life makes a man want to go back and do some of it again.

Maybe I'll get another chance with Danny after all. Lord, make it right between us. Tell me what to say and how to say it. Help me not to be too disappointed if he decides not to show up. At least I've still got Michael and JoEllen.

And while you're at it, could You take away this metal taste in my mouth? All my food tastes like I'm sucking a chain-link fence post.

Well, I'm running out of steam here, so I'd better quit writing. More tomorrow, I guess. Probably should talk to You more than once a day since You seem to have made this breakthrough with Danny.

Anyways, thanks again.
Amen.

Trisha writes...

Thanks, Lord, for Marcy. She's going to do a little shopping and then visit a friend while I'm getting my treatment. It's nice to know I'm not putting her out.

The nurse just brought a little boy into our room. She's settling him into a recliner. He looks so small, the chair seems to swallow him up. Surely he's not one of us. Maybe he's the nurse's son, and she couldn't find a sitter so she had to bring him to work with her.

She's hooking him up to a bag. Don't tell me that little one is going through this. Why isn't he in the pediatrics unit? He has to be terrified.

The guy who's never said a word to anyone is talking to the little boy. I guess wonders never cease. He introduced himself as Louis. I heard the nurse say the kid's name is Luke.

They're conversing very quietly. Must be a male thing. Little Luke didn't even whimper when the nurse stuck him with the needle.

Louis just turned his head away and closed his eyes. He looks tired. I think I'll take a turn at helping distract the boy.

"Hi, Luke. I'm Trisha."

"Hi."

"I've got one of those things too, see?" I pulled the collar down on my blouse.

"Uh-huh."

"Mine feels like a Lego block under my skin. What does yours feel like?"

"I don't know."

My heart broke. His voice was so quiet and small.

"I like to pretend it's the very top block of a very tall castle that's inside me. When the nurse puts in the medicine, I pretend that it travels down through the castle walls into all the pipes in the castle, and that all the little soldiers who live in the castle drink it like a special water every time they turn the faucets on."

The corners of his mouth turned upward in a timid grin.

"After they drink the special water, the tiny soldiers travel all through my body, and they work very hard at getting rid of all the things that make me sick. They search out every corner, even between my toes!"

He looked at his feet. "Do you think they look inside bones?"

"You can count on it. In fact, I think that's the first place they look."

"Good. Because I think that's where all the bad things are hiding." He looked up at me, his eyes misty. "How do you think they get rid of all the things that make us sick?"

The Cowardly Lion

"Well, that's the most exciting part," I said, infusing my voice with as much enthusiasm as I could muster. "When they meet the bad guys, the soldiers smile as big as they can, and all their good feelings cover up the bad guys like a big, heavy blanket. Because the bad guys don't know what to do with good feelings, they become frozen! And that gives the soldiers a chance to tie up the blanket with the bad guys inside."

I thought I heard him giggle.

"Then they take the bad guys and throw them into a clear, beautiful, flowing stream. That's why it's so important for us to drink a lot of water. It helps the soldiers keep the bad guys moving out. It's also important for us to smile a lot, because that helps the solders smile more so they can freeze more bad guys."

Luke's eyes sparkled. "I'm going to help the soldiers as much as I can. Then maybe I'll be well before Christmas gets here."

"Good for you!" I glanced at Louis. His eyes were still closed. It could've been my imagination but I thought I detected the hint of a smirk on his face. I hope he heard every word.

I don't know if little Luke will be back to our clinic. But in case he does, I'll have to come up with some more visual picture-stories to keep him feeling brave. I want to help him realize he's not alone in this. Especially since he has to be in here with a bunch of adults.

Lord, help me stay strong for Luke. Let him beat this disease and live to be a hundred. It'd be great if You could let that happen to me too. Thanks for the chance to make even this horrible disease tolerable with a little light-hearted humor.

In Jesus' name.

                       Amen.

Luke writes…

Hi, Jesus.

Today I went to the docters for medisin. I talked to a man and a lady. Mister Louis and Miss Trisha. They are nice. The lady told me what I need to do to help the medisin work. She says if I smile a lot and drink lots of water, I will help the soljers find the bad guys that are making me sick and tired.

I hope she knows what she's talking about. I figger I'll do what she says. Maybe it will help some.

I'm feeling pretty tired now. Guess I'll smile some more, drink another glass of water, and go to bed. Mom says I go to the docters again tomorrow.

Thank You, Jesus, for getting me the medisin. Help my soljers catch all the bad guys in my bones and throw them in the water and get them out of me. I figger You know all the places they mite be hiding.

You're a really good guy, Jesus.

                    Your friend,
                    Luke

Something to Think About: Chemo Courage

The big red nylon bag swished against my side. I wouldn't dream of going to chemotherapy without it. Somehow its contents gave me courage. It almost made me look forward to chemo days.

Almost.

I had received it as a thank-you gift from the store where I purchased my wig. What an unexpected surprise that store had been. Caring people, who had walked a path similar to the one I was traveling, owned and operated the little shop. In every corner I found special items to make the journey smoother.

Whenever I packed my oasis bag, I said to myself, "I have seven whole hours to do whatever I want. What will I need?" Usually, the contents included:

- Water bottles
- A book to read, either a juicy novel or a collection of inspirational thoughts
- Exercise squeeze ball for my hands or feet
- Healthy snacks (and unhealthy candy for when low moods hit)
- Chewing gum to combat the metallic taste caused by the medications
- Letters and cards to answer or reread
- A New Testament with Psalms and Proverbs
- An extra jacket or cozy sweater for when the chills came
- Phone numbers
- Lip gloss and hand cream with fragrant smells to cover the medication odors
- Small pillow to dream on
- Writing paper or a journal, with unique pen, to capture thoughts

Simply carrying that red bag made me feel more supported and less alone.

Today, I needed every ounce of support I could get. I would begin a new treatment, with a new drug, more toxic than the one I had just completed. And, I hoped, more effective. It would be infused over the course of several hours.

I checked the bag. I was not only ready, but actually anticipating the time to pamper myself. What an unusual idea—to think only about what I wanted to think about. To eat only what I wanted to eat. To read only what I wanted to read. To talk to people only when I felt like talking. To rest my head on a dreaming pillow and let it carry me away into a world of harmonious health and hope.

Instead of telling myself I was heading to the clinic, I pretended I was going to the spa, where I could indulge my every whim for hours on end.

When I arrived at the clinic, I was ready. I pushed the elevator button and, with most of my heart, I thanked God for my oasis bag of courage and for chemotherapy days. With the rest of my heart, I pretended I was going to Acapulco.

CHAPTER SEVEN

The Journey to the Great Oz

The travelers came to a place where they had to cross a big ditch. It was not possible to climb down the sides. So the lion made mighty leaps across it, each time with one of the others on his back.

After reaching safety, they were chased by monsters called Kalidahs to another huge ditch, which the lion knew he could not leap across. The tin woodsman chopped down a tree to form a bridge over it, and the Scarecrow thought of chopping away the bridge when the Kalidahs were on it.

Thus, the travelers reached safety and slept under the trees for the evening, with Dorothy dreaming of home.

Fears explored are fears faced.

One day spent in your house, this beautiful place of worship, beats thousands spent on Greek island beaches. I'd rather scrub floors in the house of my God than be honored as a guest in the palace of sin.

—Psalm 84:10

Louis writes...

Well, Lord, You've done it. Danny's coming home this weekend. Thank You, thank You, thank You! I have to say, though, I'm more than a little nervous about this whole thing. Jan's worked herself into a tizzy, planning a backyard picnic for the entire family Saturday afternoon. We're doing hamburgers, hot dogs, two kinds of potato salad, macaroni salad, fruit salad, baked beans, chips, cookies for the kids, and now she's stuck on what dessert to make for the grown-ups.

Jan and I have become "the folks." Used to be my mom and dad and her mom and dad were "the folks." Guess that means we're old.

I know I'm feeling old today. This chemo is tiring. Unbelievably so. Jan thinks she's tired after running around buying groceries and cleaning house. I used to think I knew what tired felt like too—until now.

Now I hate to think about getting up out of a chair. I wipe my face on the back of my hand because the napkins are way across the kitchen on the counter. I watch the same channel on television for hours because the remote control is on the coffee table, a whole two feet away from me. I pull my pants on each morning and then sit down to rest before I tackle shoes and socks. I'd rather eat applesauce than a crisp, juicy apple because it's too much effort to bite and chew.

I heard chemotherapy could knock the wind out of a man's sails, but I didn't know it could capsize the whole boat. I only hope I can keep myself going until after this family picnic. Jan would kill me if I laid in the bedroom all afternoon with everybody out in the yard.

I asked her what would happen if it rained Saturday afternoon. She said, "God wouldn't dare." She's getting a little gutsy in her old age, wouldn't You say, Lord?

But it would be nice if You could see to it that we had nice weather.

The Journey to the Great Oz

I'm beating around the bush here, Lord. I might as well come right out and say it. I'm scared out of my mind to face my own boy. What am I going to say to him? How do I begin to make up for all the time I wasted?

Truth is, I can't. I suppose the smartest thing to do would be to start over. I'll tell him I'm sorry and see where it goes from there. Can't say I've ever understood this forgiveness thing until now. I hope and pray he will forgive me my stupidity and let me get to know him.

Guess that goes for You too, Lord. Can you forgive me my stupidity and let me get to know You? I don't know why I kept pushing You away, except that You can be a little…big. Never figured I'd measure up, so why try? Maybe that's what Danny figured too.

Now I finally realize that measuring up isn't the issue. I'd love that boy no different if he were president of the United States or if he mowed grass for a living. Perhaps I'll tell him so one day.

I often think about one night when he was a baby. Jan was dead asleep and Danny was crying. I picked him up from his crib and held him to my chest. He pushed his little fists against me as if he knew I wasn't the right person to be holding him. Never felt so useless in my entire life. He finally settled down and let me rock him back to sleep. I wanted to sit in that rocker forever, with his hot and sweaty little head nuzzled into me.

I don't imagine I'll ever have the guts to tell him that story. Probably never get up the nerve to tell him I love him either. Men don't talk like that. I wonder why. Maybe it's because we don't want to deal with all the butterflies like I've got jammed in my stomach right now.

It's a shame, really. Life is too short to hide feelings.

Reckon I'll finish my prayers now. I'm not too good at signing off my prayers. Seems like there should be something before the amen.

Please help Danny get home safe and make him realize I did the best I could.

Well…almost the best I could.

Amen.

Trisha writes…

Heavenly Father,

The surgeon said they think they got all the cancer out of me. So why do I still feel unsettled? Am I being less than rational and allowing my fears to get the best of me?

Troy won't even talk about the possibility of more cancer. He insists we will be finished with this mess in a few months. He doesn't understand. It will never be finished. I will forever be checking my remaining breast. I will analyze every minor ache and pain and will always wonder if the cancer's back.

I also don't think I'll ever stop fighting back tears and lumps in my throat whenever I look at him and our son together. I am full of the joy of life—with the sheer bliss of knowing he and I created this family. Every day is special. Each golden moment a gift.

Bittersweet blessings, I guess you could call them. Because mixed among the moments of joy is a glittering silver thread of sadness. The consciousness of time passing is coloring the picture of my life.

Lord, I know You've prepared a room for me in heaven. I've been hearing about it my entire life. I know it is going to be incredible beyond description. Yet right now, my mind cannot accept the idea of heaven because I know I will be apart from Troy and Steven for a time. How can heaven be "heavenly" without seeing the people I love?

Lord, it's not the cancer I'm worried about now. Cancer is only one disease out of millions. If I didn't have that there would be something else. Even Your timing on this doesn't matter…not really. This is happening about forty years

The Journey to the Great Oz

earlier than I thought it would be, but in the space of eternity, forty years is like a grain of sand on a beach.

I think what I'm most bothered about is that I lose the chance to be absolutely sure Troy and Steven are coming right behind me. I know they both love You and more than likely will be fine. But I'd like to be sure. I'd like to be here to make certain they grow closer to You.

Whatever You decide, Lord, will be right for all of us. When You bring me home, life will continue here at the house. Troy will set out Steven's clothes for Sunday church services. He will put a check in the offering envelope. Steven will complain a little about having to get up early on a weekend. Life will go on.

But would You please make sure they never lose sight of heaven?

It's the only thing that truly matters.

I'm not sure why I'm talking to You like this today. Everything seems to be going fine. It's just a feeling I have...

Thanks for listening, Lord.
      Amen.

Luke writes...

Dear Jesus,

I have a question. Why doesn't the new medisin stop me from being tired? I thought it was supposed to make me well. It's not working.

I'm drinking plenty of water. I'm smiling. What else do the soljers need to find the bad guys?

Please make me well enuf to run again. I miss running.

Thank You.
      Your friend,
      Luke

P.S. Sorry I don't feel like talking longer. I'm just too tired.

Something to Think About: Fatigue and Fear

Leave It to Beaver droned on the television, providing some relief to the monotony of endless days of inactivity. I longed for the day when I would feel halfway like myself again. I tried to think positively, to maintain a good attitude. I knew I was learning some valuable lessons, lessons I would not have learned any other way.

One lesson was staring me in the face at that very moment. A mere foot and a half away, on the coffee table, sat the remote control for the TV. My thoughtful husband had carefully made me cozy on the sofa and had placed the remote and a glass of ice water where he thought it would be easy for me to reach. He didn't know that the foot and a half may as well have been five miles.

Too far, my body screamed when I thought about reaching for it. *Too heavy*, my body screamed as I moved my arm slightly. *Too tired.* My mind reeled with the mental effort of moving.

I coveted my lost energy.

So that's what *covet* means, I thought. I would give anything to have a portion of my energy back. Well, I would do anything...if only I had the energy.

I grinned at the irony of my thoughts. I imagined picking up the remote. I imagined changing the channel. I imagined returning it to its place on the table. I imagined taking a sip of cool water. It was nearly as good as the real thing.

But *Leave it to Beaver* droned on.

CHAPTER EIGHT

The Deadly Poppy Fields

The travelers awoke full of hope. As they continued their journey, they found themselves in a meadow of deadly red poppies. Anyone who breathed the aroma of the flowers would fall asleep and eventually die. The tin woodsman and the scarecrow were immune as they were not made of flesh. They carried Dorothy and Toto to safety, but had to leave the sleeping lion behind because he was too heavy to carry.

The deadly flower bed of depression can be overcome when loving hands carry you away from its malicious odor.

> God holds me head and shoulders above all who try to pull me down. I'm headed for his place to offer anthems that will raise the roof! Already I'm singing God-songs; I'm making music to God.
> —Psalm 27:6

Louis writes…

> Dear Lord,
> Oh, how I wish I could turn back the clock! Back to when Danny was a little boy. Back to before the other kids were born. Maybe if I started at the beginning, I could do a better job of being a father.

The Saturday backyard picnic didn't go well. Everyone showed up and the food was good and it didn't rain, but it was all wrong somehow—like we were out of practice at being a family. Michael must have told his children to behave because they sat around as if they were afraid to move. JoEllen tried to keep the conversation going by talking about subjects nobody could argue over. Nobody could argue because nobody knew anything about them.

Jan tried to break the ice by pushing food at everyone. A person can only eat a certain amount till they run out of room.

It was like we were wearing our best manners. Or like we had Sunday clothes on and couldn't wait for church to be over so we could rush home and put on our jeans. The whole day felt stiff and uncomfortable. And Danny...well...

He and the family got in late Friday night. Jan picked them up at the airport. I had butterflies in my stomach the whole time she was gone. Must have gone to the bathroom about six times. When they pulled in the driveway, I had this wild urge to run out the back door. Of course, I didn't. Jan would have locked it after me and I'd still be trying to get back inside.

Danny walked up the front walk. He was arm in arm with Jan...wish it could have been my arm. They came in...wife and kids too...and just stood there and smiled.

I didn't know what to say or do. So I stood there and smiled too. Should have hugged him, but I couldn't do it. I guess I was disappointed he didn't hug me first.

"How was your flight?" I asked him.

"Pretty smooth."

"Get all your baggage?"

"Yes. It all came through okay."

I couldn't stand it any longer. I thrust my hand out to him. "Glad you're home, Son."

"Me too."

He took my hand, grasped it firmly, and held my fingers a bit longer than necessary. His hands felt strong, sure, and capable. He had grown up. And probably wasn't going to be giving me much more than a handshake until I'd earned it.

Jan took over and bustled everyone upstairs to their rooms, showing them around.

Saturday we did some more bustling, getting things ready for the picnic. I thought I had made a breakthrough while we were cleaning the grill. Danny came out as I started scrubbing the rack.

"Hey, Dad," he said. "Let me do that for you."

"Oh. Okay." I handed him the brush.

He began scrubbing. "How have you been feeling?" His eyes didn't look up from the rack.

"Oh, I have good days and some not-so-good days."

He nodded, as if he expected the answer. "Too bad we're not closer."

I wondered if he meant closer in distance or closer to each other.

"Can't help you out much when we're across the country."

"Nope, guess not." I hesitated. "It'd be good to get a phone call once in a while, though."

He glanced up at me. "Same goes for me."

I nodded.

He finished scrubbing the grill and handed it to me.

"Thanks," I said.

And that was it. I've been kicking myself ever since. What is wrong with me? I can't seem to come right out and say what I'm thinking. Why couldn't I tell him I was sorry for hurting him? That I'd made a huge mistake? It's like the words get all jumbled up in my head and stick in my throat, and I can't think of what I want to say until the chance to say them is past.

I had no problem telling Danny what to do when he was a kid. I was issuing orders then, not really talking. Maybe that's the best I can do. But I don't want it to be. I want to know him…like a father should know his son.

But now he's gone back home across the country. And I don't know when he's coming back. I feel like I swallowed a rock.

Help me, Lord.
Amen.

Trisha writes…

Lord,

I feel as if I'm living two lives at the same time. One life is in front of family, friends, and people in general. The Trisha they know is strong, courageous, optimistic, and cheerful. She puts the best spin on everything because it seems to help them, and it's what they expect from her.

The other life is me when I'm by myself. Nobody knows that Trisha…except You, Lord. I'm not eager to share her with anyone else. Partly because I'm just getting to know her myself. This cancer is teaching me to look deeper, to take time to figure out who I really am. It's strange that I've never done it before now…at least not in this way.

I'm beginning to separate the real me from the physical me. I have discovered if someone peeled away my skin and bones, I would still be there. I am more than a body. While the cancer happening to my physical self is terrible, it can't touch the real me. And that's why this will never be the crisis people make it out to be.

As each day passes, my assurance grows. I am sure You love me, I am sure I will be okay one way or another, and I am sure You will use this opportunity to bring others closer to You.

I am praying the "others" includes Troy and Steven. I wish I could find words to take away their fears. I hope I have a chance to talk with them about this. If I die from this, I want it to count for something.

It's interesting to hear what people say when they come to visit me. Some ask, "How are you doing?" as soon as they step in the door. They say it in a way that makes me think they'd like to add "you poor thing" on the end of the sentence. Others say, "You're looking well," as if I'm a gullible three-year-old. Some don't even acknowledge I am there. They just visit with Troy and Steven.

I wish they felt secure enough to say, "Tell me how it's going," and stick around to listen to the answer. I know they want to say and do the right thing. I wish I had the courage to help them learn. For the most part, I give them the standard answer: "I'm okay. Thanks for asking." Then I flash them a smile so they can leave feeling as if they've done their duty.

After everyone's gone, I sink into my pillow and become the other me...the one You know so well—the tired one, the one for whom smiling is an effort. I know I'm sounding like a whiny child here, Lord, but that's how I feel.

It would be easy to let my guard down and slip into the wonderfully numb state of depression. I wouldn't have to react to anything. Before this is all over, it will probably happen. Most of the research I've read says depression is common and expected at some point during chronic illness. I guess I need to be ready for it.

Thanks for sticking with me, Lord. Thanks for letting me show my other side to You, and for loving me, holding me, and being patient with me as I figure some of this out. I never knew being sick could be this challenging. If You allow me to work as a nurse again, I pray I will never forget these lessons I'm learning. Sick people should be allowed to be themselves and not have to use precious energy trying to be what others expect them to be.

My head is spinning. It's time to crawl into Your arms and rest awhile.

I love You, Lord. Amen.

Luke writes…

Dear Jesus,

I can't hear You talking. Will you pleese talk to me? Tell me why I'm not well enuf to play soccer yet. I am helping the soljers fight the bad guys as much as I can. I drink lots of water.

But I'm tired of smiling. Miss Trish seems tired of smiling too. Mr. Louis never smiled much to begin with, so his soljers probly need a lot of help. Can you pleese give us some other ideas to help us?

Mommy's working a lot and she's not smiling much either. She says to do what the docters say and Im doing it but it's not working. I get pooped when I walk down the hall to the big chair between Miss Trish and Mr. Louis.

And the guys put Curtis on the team in my place.

I know You must have more ideas for us. Would You please talk louder so we can hear You? We will lissen hard. I promise.

               Love,
               Luke

Something to Think About: The Unseen Battle

I envisioned microscopic red and blue soldiers standing shoulder to shoulder, lining the sides of my blood vessels. The red soldiers held broad shields. They prevented the incoming chemicals from attacking my healthy cells. The blue soldiers pointed out the hiding places of the cancer cells in my body, enabling the medicine to quickly find and destroy every damaging cell.

When I first began the imaginary battle, I thought myself somewhat silly, but it soon became essential. I willed my body into action and I felt that it gave the chemotherapy an added effectiveness.

I closed my eyes and leaned back into the recliner. I needed another pillow behind my back, and a blanket, too, but the nurse was busy with someone else. I sighed as the chemicals continued their trek from the intravenous bag into my body.

The imaginary battle raged. In my mind, the toxic chemicals became big cartoon-like blobs with huge mouths and sharp teeth, always moving, always searching for something to swallow. I prayed with my whole body.

God, let them find and destroy every cancer cell in me. Help the blue soldiers point out every hiding place. Don't let any cancer cells escape them. Let the red soldiers stand strong. United, tough. Give them endurance to withstand the continuing attacks.

I sighed again.

Am I being silly, Lord? Imagining a battle? It feels like a battle. I fight to stand up in the morning. I fight to make it to the bathroom. I fight for the energy to brush my teeth, to wash my face. I fight to exist through these endless days.

And then I heard Him speak.

You're not silly. But instead of fighting to endure, you must fight to triumph. Fight to smile. Fight to see My gifts for you. Fight to see inside the hearts of those around you. Fight to help them grow. Fight to grow yourself. I have much to give you, both now and later. I've given you a mind and a soul. Use them! Fight to find joy in spite of the circumstances. Fight to see Me, for I will never leave your side.

With a quiet smile, I let His Spirit encircle me.

The war of chronic illness has a variety of battlefields. Much of the fighting occurs unobserved. From the onlooker's vantage point, the ill person appears to be resting with closed eyes. But inside the mind, ammunition is being volleyed from side to side as thoughts and feelings are thrown around like hand grenades and javelins.

Some of the greatest triumphs with disease come when lying quietly on a pillow. God has given us imaginations to use to the best of our abilities. As treatment progresses, battles may grow even more detailed, adding strength and comfort to the weary soldier.

Paul tells us in 2 Corinthians 4:18, "There's far more here than meets the eye. The things we see now are here today, gone tomorrow. But the things we can't see now will last forever." The unseen battle is truly eternal. If we're not fighting cancer or a chronic illness, we are fighting something else. Much of the time we fight ourselves, our weaknesses, and our earthly desires.

We need never feel as if we are fighting alone. Or as if we are fighting without hope. We can always depend on the strength of the Savior to surround us. We can face any battle knowing the ultimate victory will be ours because He has won it for us.

Fighting alone, without Him, only exhausts us, and it disappoints God greatly. He will stand by with a sorrowful face and tears in His eyes as He sees our pain and futile efforts, waiting for us to ask for His help.

So ask Him.

CHAPTER NINE

The Queen of the Field Mice

The tin woodsman rescued the travelers and a gray field mouse from a strange beast. The mouse happened to be the Queen of all Field Mice. Out of her gratitude, she ordered the mice to carry out the tin woodsman's wishes. The woodsman built a truck and had the field mice pull the lion out of the deadly poppy field to safety.

Trust means simply trust…not do, not fix, not plan, not manipulate. Only trust.

> You keep me going when times are tough—my bedrock, God, since my childhood. I've hung on you from the day of my birth, the day you took me from the cradle; I'll never run out of praise. Many gasp in alarm when they see me, but you take me in stride.
>
> —Psalm 71:5–7

Louis writes…

> Dear Lord,
> The kids aren't paying much attention to what I'm going through because they don't see anything happening. I have

the feeling when they first heard I had "it," they expected me to keel over and die right away. When nothing seemed to change, at least on the outside, they figured it was no big deal.

Michael stops by the house once a week, but that's what he did before, so that's no different. JoEllen only calls and asks Jan if I've been to church. She probably figures she's done her duty. Danny's back on the coast so I figure I won't see more of him until I'm close to dying…if that's what You have planned for me. Even Jan seems like she doesn't care much. She's going about her usual routine, running here and there, doing her housework, visiting friends, shopping.

My life consists of doctor visits, chemo treatments, standing in line at the pharmacy, and resting. A big nothing of a life. I feel as if I know the folks in the clinic room better than my own family. Is this how it's supposed to be? No wonder people shrivel up into nothing with this.

Speaking of shriveling, that little guy, Luke, is not doing well at all. He was tiny to begin with, and now he's grown so thin he's nearly invisible. Having a hard time breathing too. Everything seems to tire him out. Can't You see Your way clear to help him out? He's only a child.

I can understand why You might not help me. My life's pretty much finished anyhow. But this little guy is barely started.

I heard him talking to that Trisha woman this morning. She seems to be pretty good with him. They were talking about You. I didn't catch it all, but I did hear Luke say he talks to You a lot and wonders why You don't talk loud enough for him to hear.

I wonder the same thing myself sometimes. Of course I'm out of practice so I guess that's the reason I don't hear You. But the poor little guy wants to hear You. Seems to me You could do something about that.

Trisha told him sometimes You talk through other people. Now he will be looking at everybody and wondering if it's You talking. Sounds ridiculous to me, but maybe it will keep him hanging on.

Every time I close my eyes I see Luke's pale little face, and I hear him wheezing, struggling for a good breath of air.

So far, I don't think much of Your answers to prayers. You can do better than this for us, can't You?

No offense.

Amen.

Trisha writes…

Lord God,

I am numb. My hair is gone everywhere from my body, even my eyelashes. My energy's gone, too, and I can't find many reasons to smile. I can barely chew and swallow food. Everything tastes like cardboard. I'm cold all the time.

Troy's walking around like a zombie. I can't tell if he's mad or sad. Steven still comes to tuck me into bed at night, but I can tell he's scared.

My whole body aches. Every movement brings pain. I walk like a ninety-year-old, shuffling slowly along. I want to sit undisturbed in a soft chair somewhere and sleep. I am tempted to quit chemo and go the natural therapy route. If I had more energy to look into it, I'd probably do it.

I want to get lost in my mind, think about heaven, and dream of painless days and warm sunshine. I cannot endure being in this state much longer.

They started me on an antidepressant today. The nurse said my serotonin levels were out of balance—a natural response to the chemo. I feel bad about having to take it though. I should be able to do this without extra drugs, shouldn't I? After all, I knew this depression would be coming. I don't know why it caught me by surprise.

Luke is failing. He's using his accessory muscles to breathe. They need to do something quickly if they're going to save that little boy. Breaks my heart…but either way, he will be with You.

We talked about You today. The little guy wants to hear Your voice. Surround him with Your love, Father. Let Him know You are there. If You take him home, please take him gently and swiftly. But we'd sure be grateful if You'd let him stay with us.

I met his mom today. They're getting ready to admit him to pediatrics ICU. Not a good sign. This is the part I've always hated about nursing. Sometimes we have to let go.

I need You as never before. I don't know what else to say. I am too tired to think. And I am almost too tired to breathe. Living seems heavy.

I love You, Lord.

Use me however You want.

My life is in Your hands…always has been. I need to sleep now.

Your child,
Trisha

Luke writes…

Jesus,
    Help me breeth.

Love,
Luke

Luke's Mom writes…

Dear God, don't let this happen! He's too young. Take somebody else, not him. Show me what to do. Help the doctors and nurses fix his breathing. He's only a baby. He's such a good boy. Let him grow up to be a good man.
Amen.

Something to Think About: Looking Death in the Face

(Note to reader: During my treatments, I remembered this incident, which occurred years earlier in my nursing career.)

I gently placed the man's lifeless arms across the bath towel and tenderly washed and dried each limb with warm water. I wondered how many times his arms had hugged his children, how many times he had playfully squeezed his wife, and how often his muscles ached with the fatigue of work. I spent extra time on his hands and fingernails, carefully removing all traces of his last battle for life, a battle he had lost. I knew his hands would be the first thing his family would want to touch, hold, and even kiss as they said their final good-byes.

Nursing was difficult. Frustrations often resulted from lack of adequate staff and long hours. An entire microcosm of life was held within each day. But I cherished every hour, considering it a privilege to help others through critical times in their lives.

Now, as I looked death in the face, intense waves of sadness flowed over me. I knew his family would soon begin to mourn.

Whether a death was sudden and unexpected or long anticipated didn't seem to make a difference. The loss would hurt. It was my job to ease the transition from grief to hope.

I combed his hair, remembering he parted it on the left side. I retrieved his wedding ring from the nightstand drawer and slid it on his finger. I placed a clean hospital gown on him and pulled the sheet and bedspread up to his chest, leaving his hands and arms ready for his family.

I dimmed the lights, taking away some of death's starkness, and turned the radio to his favorite country music station, playing softly. Then I prayed, thanking God for the privilege of taking care of one of His children.

> This is the testimony in essence: God gave us eternal life; the life is in his Son. So, whoever has the Son, has life; whoever rejects the Son, rejects life.
>
> —1 John 5:11–12

It doesn't get any plainer than this. Through the agonizing days of an ongoing illness, when we are not able to see how or when life will end, we can embrace the reality of hope. Whether the hope is for life or for death doesn't matter. Our hope is Jesus Christ. He is with us in life. He is with us in death. He is with us forever.

CHAPTER TEN

The Guardian of the Gates

The cowardly lion finally awakened after breathing the fresh air. Dorothy and her fellow travelers once again found the yellow brick road and headed toward the Emerald City, where the Wizard of Oz lived. They spent the night with a farmer and his family who had been to the Emerald City several times, but had never seen the wizard. They had heard he had plenty of brains to share, a collection of hearts, and a pot of courage in his throne room.

When they reached the city, the Guardian of the Gates placed green eyeglasses on them to shield their eyes from the brightness of the city. He then unlocked the gate so they could enter.

Heaven on earth can be visualized if we will only consent to wearing heavenly colored glasses.

> But there's far more to life for us. We're citizens of high heaven! We're waiting the arrival of the Savior, the Master, Jesus Christ, who will transform our earthly bodies into glorious bodies like his own. He'll make us beautiful and whole with the same powerful skill by which he is putting everything as it should be, under and around him.
> —Philippians 3:20–21

Louis writes...

Dear Lord,

    I guess You know they took little Luke to the hospital. His mom was barely holding herself together. I don't blame her.

    The doctors aren't telling us what's going on with him, so I'm sure it's not good. Hope he makes it. He didn't take up much space in that big recliner, but it sure looks empty now.

    I never had to go through losing one of my kids. Thank You for that. Sorry if I seemed spiteful yesterday. I'm upset about the boy. I'm not real happy about my family either. If being this sick doesn't make them want to get to know me, nothing will.

    I suppose I need to make more of an effort. They're young. They don't know how fast life goes. We're born, we live, we die. That's it, I guess, except for the heaven part afterward. I'm not real sure that will be as great as everybody says it will. How do they know anyway? I only hope You haven't sold us a bill of goods.

    I hate being sick. I'm coughing like crazy. Feel like an old worn-out Ford, choking and sputtering all the time. Chemo's messing up everything in my body. Can't hardly eat what Jan fixes and I think she takes it personally when I push the plate away. She just doesn't know.

    And now I've got this problem on the other end. I'm getting calluses from sitting in the bathroom so long. My legs get so numb I can hardly stand up afterward. I've tried everything. This morning I sat there nearly an hour trying to get things going, and had no luck at all. Feels like I'm trying to push a piano through a porthole.

    I sat beside Trisha at chemo today. Seems like a nice enough person. I guess her being a nurse makes it easier to handle this kind of stuff. For a minute or two, I almost felt like telling her about my bathroom problem, thinking she might know a trick or two. But I caught myself before I did. Doesn't seem right for a man to tell a lady such a thing.

Although if she wasn't sick, and happened to be my nurse, I'd probably tell her. She's that kind of person.

She's worried about Luke too. I've been thinking about him more than my own kids these past two days. I told her there's nothing we can do. She disagreed. She said we need to pray harder. So I guess I'll do my part. Here goes…

Lord, please don't take him away. Let the little guy make it. He should get a chance to grow up. I don't know what Your heaven will be like. A lot of people are counting on it being great. Even if that's so, Luke ought to have a run at being a teenager and a grown-up first.

That's about all I have to say.
Amen.

Trisha writes…

Dear Lord,

How much worse will it get? I'd just like to know. I can't help but question Your level of goodness when You allow Luke to suffer like this. It's frightening for a child not to be able to catch his breath…for an adult too. I'm glad we don't have to watch him deteriorate, but it's not making it any easier.

Other than my sorrow for Luke, I don't seem to have enough energy to feel anything. It's as if someone has injected my heart with Novocain. Nothing hurts. And nothing makes me happy either. I can barely remember what it's like to feel happy. This antidepressant med will take about two weeks before I experience any benefits. Maybe that's a good thing. Maybe Luke will be through this crisis by then.

I want to believe You are in control of this. I want to believe You have a master plan. I just want to believe. But right now, I'm too tired.

And You know what? Right now, I really don't care.

I don't want to do this anymore. Make it all go away. I'm tired of telling others to pray and everything will be fine.

Because maybe it won't.

Do you really need an amen?

Something to Think About: Little Victories

Stool softeners, laxatives, and fiber supplements lined the bottom shelf to the left of the kitchen sink. Other medications graced the shelf as well, but the presence of these three bothered me greatly.

Only old people should need these. I roughly grabbed the bottles and slammed them down on the counter. Even after I had endured the rigor of a day's activities, I had to face my inability to control my body's most basic functions. Chemotherapy had taken away more than my hair and my energy. It had robbed my body of one of its most natural and necessary expressions. I swallowed the recommended doses, replaced the bottles, and said, "Okay, pills, do your thing."

The next morning, while it was still dark, I groped my way to the bathroom, imagining great success. As I sat in the dark, I received nothing more than another lesson in patience.

I flipped on the light switch. Maybe distraction would help. I picked up a magazine. No good. I couldn't read with my eyes squeezed shut. Back to the mind game. If I could relax my muscles enough, I knew this could work.

Following a long and hard-fought battle, success was finally achieved!

Greatly weakened from the effort, I stumbled back to bed and grinned as I pulled the covers over myself. *That felt better than winning the lottery.*

Little victories. Humbling, exhausting, and very basic, but still a victory. It counted.

From agonizing constipation to full-blown depression, each new side road of chronic illness colors perceptions of heaven. Depending on the color of glasses we look through, the world can turn from sunshine yellow to midnight black in hours or even minutes.

Supportive family members realize that the most dramatic changes are due to the illness and not to individual decisions. Continuing to offer understanding and love in spite of radical mood changes is the goal. It stands as a monumental challenge.

Paul encourages both caregivers and sick family members with these words: "My grace is enough; it's all you need. My strength comes into its own in your weakness" (2 Corinthians 12:9).

As I endured the days of treatment and therapy, I experienced new depths of both weakness and grace. Everyday tasks such as brushing my teeth seemed as unattainable as climbing Mount Everest. To accomplish this great feat, I had to stand, walk to the sink, find the toothbrush and toothpaste, unscrew the cap from the tube, hold the brush up while putting the toothpaste on it, put the brush down, screw the cap back on the toothpaste, pick the brush back up, lean over the sink, turn on the faucet, brush my teeth, spit, rinse the brush, brush teeth again, spit, rinse the brush, put it away, turn off the faucet, wipe my face with a towel, and somehow find the energy to walk back to the sofa or bed. Simply thinking about it exhausted me.

The sentence that echoed in my mind during this time was "I can't believe a person can be this tired and still be alive." I kept reminding myself to remember feeling this way. I didn't want to forget it because if I did recover, I wanted to deeply appreciate every small activity and every particle of life I was given.

The Bible says, "We carry this precious Message around in the unadorned clay pots of our ordinary lives" (2 Corinthians 4:7). When we realize that the source of life's power is God, a dazzling, brilliant awareness is unveiled. Life is a treasure. Every bit of it. Breathing, moving, lifting, brushing, even spitting is a gift.

The journey to reach this truth is convoluted. Nothing is of greater help to the suffering traveler than to have family and friends as pleasant, supportive company. With more than one set of hands on the steering wheel, the twists and turns of the road are easier to navigate.

CHAPTER ELEVEN

The Emerald City of Oz

All of the travelers had private audiences with the Wizard of Oz. Each one saw the wizard in a different form. Dorothy saw a huge head. The scarecrow saw a lovely lady. The tin woodsman saw a terrible beast. The Lion saw a ball of fire.

The wizard told them he would grant their wishes, but only if one of them would kill the Wicked Witch of the West. This seemed an impossible task for the travelers and it worried them greatly.

Looking for help anywhere other than where Jesus directs you is a waste of time.

> Jesus said, "I am the Road, also the Truth, also the Life. No one gets to the Father apart from me."
> —John 14:6

Louis writes...

Dear Lord,
Do You see where I am today? I am on my knees. My arms are wrapped around this toilet bowl. I figured since I was in this position anyway I'd have a few words with You. This dang-blasted chemo can't be working right.

I've got the door locked so Jan won't barge in. She's been pounding on it for about fifteen minutes now, wanting me to let her inside. She means well, but she'd be hauling me off to the doctor if she saw me like this. I figure the doctors are the ones who got me into this mess in the first place. Best to stay away and let the old body work through it alone.

Every time I put something in my mouth it comes right back up...or right out the other end. None of that vomit medicine seems to work. And this diarrhea is about to send me over the edge. First I can't go at all, then I get really excited that things are happening again, and now I can't seem to stop it. Settling this down is going to keep me occupied the rest of the day. If I weren't so weak I wouldn't be worried, but look at my hands—they're shaking.

Wonder what the little guy is going through today. And I wonder where his daddy is. I got the impression there wasn't a father in the picture. Doesn't seem right not to have a dad to help him over the rough spots. It's been about a week now since we've seen the boy. Maybe he'll be back before too long. I figure no news is good news where he's concerned.

I hear the phone ringing. Good. It will give Jan something to do. I feel so weak. Maybe I'll just lie down here on the cool tile floor for a while. Oh, for Pete's sake. Jan's knocking on the door again.

"What do you want?"

"Honey, you've got to come out and talk on the phone. It's Danny! He wants to talk to you."

Danny? Why would he want to talk to me when he can talk to his mother?

"Honey, it's long distance. He's waiting for you."

"All right, all right. Give me another minute."

I can't believe Danny wants to talk to me.

"Danny? Is that you?"

"Yes, Dad, it's me."

"Anything the matter?"

"No, not really. I just thought I'd call and see if it'd be okay if I came and spent some time with you."

"Why? Never mind, don't answer that."

"I've got a man here at work to cover for me, so I can come pretty soon, if it's okay with you."

"Fine, Son. You just come right on ahead. You're not going to drive all the way from California, are you?"

"No, I'll be flying. I'll see you soon then?"

"I'll be here...at least I think I will be."

"Okay, Dad. Bye."

"Good-bye, Son."

Can you beat that? Danny...coming here to spend time with me. I guess maybe You've been hearing me pray after all, Lord. Thanks.

Guess I'd better go rest up. My son's coming to town.
                Amen.

Trisha writes...

Father,

I feel like a small child. I long to curl up in Your arms. I ache to hear Your voice. I think You must sound like my father sounded when I was little and I cuddled up in his arms. He would hold me against him and his voice was deep and comforting. I could feel it vibrate through his chest against my ear. It sounded strong and protective.

I am so hot. Everything on me is red and throbbing. I'm not going to check my temperature because I know I'm way too hot. I took some Tylenol but it's not working yet. Even my eyes are hot. Please make this heat go away.

I keep turning this pillow over, but it's hot on both sides. There is no cool spot left in this bed. I need to get up and put some water in the tub and soak awhile, but I'm too hot to move. I can't imagine why I'm having a fever...infection maybe? But where? I don't know...I'm too hot to think.

I heard Troy and Steven tiptoe in to check on me. He told Steven to leave me alone and let me sleep. Sleep! I can't sleep. I can't talk. I'm just too hot. I need ice, water, cool sheets, a fan, somebody to take these covers off me...Lord, please send someone who knows what I need without my having to ask.

I bet heaven is cool. Gentle winds must blow there all the time. Soft songs probably ride on the breezes. I want to go to heaven, Lord.

Now.

Troy would be okay. Steven will be okay too. I want to hear Your voice. I want to curl up in Your arms. You would put a cool cloth on my head that would never get hot.

Please?

Amen.

Luke writes...

Dear Jesus,

I think I'm ready to go home. These people are nice, but I want my own bed and pillo. I can breeth okay. Let me go home.

Pleese?

Your frend,
Luke

Something to Think About: The Heat of Battle

Dry, scorching heat consumed my body. I longed to move my legs to search out a cooler part of the bed, but whenever I moved, pain overtook me. I thought about calling out for a cool cloth, but my dry throat couldn't work up enough saliva to speak. The oppressive heat enveloped my body like a heavy, hooded winter coat.

I had been lovingly and properly nursed and medicated and I knew I just had to wait until the soothing measures took effect.

I imagined my thoughts written on three-dimensional pages. I turned to the first page, eager to read what was written there.

But the words on the pages refused to stay in straight lines. Images of flames and deserts interrupted the sentences. Question marks popped up out of nowhere. Jumbled thoughts and rambling questions bounced from the page and landed directly in front of me, demanding answers.

Why am I sick? Why is it so hot? Will I ever feel good again? Why doesn't somebody bring me something cold? How long can this go on? Why is my body too heavy to move? If I'm going to die, why won't my mind fall asleep? Please, God, let me just fall asleep. Will this ever end?

What am I supposed to be learning from this? Lord God, I don't think I can bear it!

Then, as suddenly as the fire came, a cooling voice spoke.

I am the real fire in you. My Spirit is glowing within you. I am changing you from the inside out. Embrace the heat like sprouting seeds welcome the sunshine. For you are a sprouting seed.

You will experience intense heat for a time, but I will not allow your spirit to be burned. I am your Father and I love you.

The battle is not only about your body. It is about you growing up into Me. And it is a battle you are winning!

I didn't feel as if I were winning. But I endured the battles, one at a time.

I appreciated the kind words and actions of my caregivers. But even with loving family members surrounding me, I felt completely alone, separated from the rest of the world.

I hungered for my Lord. And He always satisfied my appetite. I clung to Him. And He never moved out of my reach. I told Him everything. And He listened to every syllable.

After a while, the battle became insignificant. My body hurt, but it didn't matter. I was hotter than I'd ever been. I knew the fighting would continue for as long as I drew breath. But I refused to let it wear me down.

All I needed, whether awake or asleep, whether in life or in death, was Him.

"The main character in this drama…will ignite the kingdom life within you, a fire within you, the Holy Spirit within you, changing you from the inside out" (Matthew 3:11).

I was being changed. And if this was how He wanted to do it, that was fine with me. I had never before tasted a depth of love such as this.

CHAPTER TWELVE

The Search for the Wicked Witch

Dorothy and the other travelers journeyed onward to find and destroy the Wicked Witch of the West. Along the way, Tin Woodsman and Scarecrow were rendered useless by the winged monkeys. Dorothy and the cowardly lion were captured and made slaves by the wicked witch. Because Dorothy carried the mark of the Good Witch's kiss on her forehead, no one could harm her, but Dorothy did not know this.

The wicked witch tried to steal one of Dorothy's magical shoes. This made Dorothy so mad she threw water on the witch, not knowing the water would make the witch melt away to nothing.

Free at last, Dorothy ran to tell the lion they were no longer prisoners in a strange land.

A single drop of water sent by God is enough to destroy the draught in the most resistant of wizened souls. Perhaps you are His drop of water.

> I'm absolutely convinced that nothing—nothing living or dead, angelic or demonic, today or tomorrow, high or low, thinkable or unthinkable—absolutely nothing can get between us and God's love because of the way that Jesus our Master has embraced us.
> —Romans 8:38–39

Louis writes...

Dear Lord,

I can't tell You how much this means to me—You sending Danny here. I know it had to be You who made it happen, because I was totally tongue-tied when he was here for that weekend with the rest of the family. I didn't know where to begin with him and I don't think he knew either.

He's been here for three days now. Doesn't seem to be in a hurry to get back. He said he has a man taking care of his business and he isn't worried about keeping things running. From the sound of it, his auto shop is doing great. We've been talking about it quite a bit. Of course we talked about his family too. If anyone had been listening, they would have thought we were two strangers just getting acquainted.

I've come to the conclusion he's turned into a good husband and father. Never thought I'd get to say that about him.

We drove over to the park yesterday. I told him I needed to see some of the world other than the doctor's offices and the pharmacy. So after lunch, he said, "Let's go for a ride, Dad." If he only knew how warm and full I feel inside when he calls me Dad.

We drove into the park a little ways, turned off the car, and walked over to the riverbank. There was a bench facing the water and I had to sit and rest. He didn't say anything, but stood awhile. Then finally he came and sat beside me. Both of us, side by side...watching the water.

"Dad?" He cleared his throat. I turned to look at him. "There are some things I need to say." His head turned back to face the water.

"Go ahead. I'm not going anywhere."

"I came back because things weren't right between us." He paused. "And I wanted to see if I could fix it."

I sat there, wondering what he was going to say next. And whether I would respond right.

"When I left, I was a kid—a stubborn, bull-headed kid who wanted his own way. Truth is, I wanted to show you up, to show you how wrong you were."

"I'd say you accomplished that, Danny," I told him. "I was wrong, I admit it. You've done real well for yourself."

"I've done okay. But I'd have done better if I'd stayed home, gone to college, listened to you..." He looked at the ground. "Anyway, I didn't want you to think I didn't love you all that time I was gone."

My eyes blurred. I turned to look at his face. "I didn't know what else to think, Son. You didn't write. You didn't ask to speak to me when you talked to your mother." I looked back at the river, a lump in my throat. "It hurt pretty deep."

"Hurt me too," he said, letting the words fade away.

We sat a bit longer, not speaking, not moving. We listened to each other breathe. We watched the river flow. We received the moment into our memories.

It's been easier since we sat on the bench and looked at the river. I've let my guard down. Too bad I didn't do it earlier.

Sometime soon I'm going to have to tell Danny about these conversations You and I keep having, Lord. Before I leave this earth, I'd like him to know it is possible to get prayers answered. You could have been a little quicker at it, but I'm not complaining. It's great to have him here.

Life could certainly be worse. This isn't so bad. So thank You.

      Amen.

Trisha writes...

Lord God,

Finally this antidepressant is kicking in. I feel "lighter" today. Two weeks is a long time to wait for changes. I was beginning to lose hope. Of course, it helped a lot to see Luke's little face back with us this morning. He's quite weak, had to be wheeled in. But he seems to be breathing much easier than the last time we saw him.

When he came in, everybody clapped! I think he was a bit embarrassed, but he grinned at all of us.

The nurses hooked us up to our fluids, we settled into our recliners, and then Louis's son from California walked through the door.

"Luke, I'd like you to meet my boy," Louis said. "His name is Danny."

"Hi."

"Hi, Luke," Danny thrust out his hand for Luke to shake. Luke lifted his hand slowly, grinning. Danny carefully held the pale, fragile fingers, engulfing them in his calloused, powerful hand.

Luke and Danny talked and laughed. They pretended to be soldiers fighting bad guys. Somehow that evolved into them becoming a pair of proud lions prowling across their land. Danny seemed at ease in the child's world of make-believe and was obviously enjoying himself.

As they played, I saw a transformation come over Louis. He observed the interaction between his son and Luke, almost with jealousy, I think. Perhaps he hadn't experienced the free-flowing exchange of ideas with Danny as a boy. Or maybe he had wanted Danny all to himself today. Anybody could see Luke and Danny had connected in a big way.

"Could I be included in your pride?" I asked, eager to part a part of their game.

"Miss Trish, you can be our lioness," Luke said with great seriousness. "But you're the only lady lion we'll let be in our pack."

"Why, thank you, Luke. I consider it a great honor."

Danny stood. "Well, I'm about to embark on a mission," he announced, laying a hand on his father's shoulder. "I'm going downstairs to the gift shop to get something for our fellow lion Louis to read. Anybody want this brave king of the jungle to get them a candy bar or some gum while I'm there?"

"Oh, yes, please," said Luke.

"Maybe you could provide us with some tall, cool bottles of pure, fortifying drinking water," I suggested.

Discreetly checking the condition of his father's wrinkled, cracked mouth, Danny added, "And some tubes of lip balm to keep our lips from drying out. It wouldn't be right for lions to have dry lips."

I reached for my purse. "Let me help finance this mission of yours today."

"Oh, no, you don't," Danny was quick to reply. "The lioness of our pride shouldn't have to worry about things like that, should she?"

They all agreed, and Danny left for his mission.

I know what You must be thinking, Lord. Silly creatures, aren't we—pretending to be lions? But I think we will need to draw on all Your gifts to endure this huge mission You have sent us on. As we use our imaginations and band together, perhaps it will make the mission a bit less burdensome. We're going to need more than water and lip balm to survive.

Give us the courage to endure, the willingness to reach out to one another, and the strength to fight when we are too tired to think. You brought us together at this time, in this place, for a reason. Use me as You will, to help these three "lions" see Your loving hand as we travel ahead.

Thank You for taking away the darkness in my outlook today. It's hard to stay depressed when I've been made the honorary "lioness" of the pride. I pray I will not let them down.

                            Amen.

Luke writes...

Dear Jesus,

I am back at the docter's place. Thanks for making me feel better. I had fun today. I made a new frend. His name is Danny. He is Mr. Louis's son even tho he is a grown-up. We talked about lions. Miss Trish is our lady lion.

Danny went on a mission for us lions. He brout me back water and a comic book and something to rub on my mouth. It smells like a coconut. I like it. I guess I gotta come back tomorrow for some more medisin, but I don't care cuz the other lions will be here too.

Anyway, thanks, Jesus, for making me breeth better and the fever go away. I don't think I'll tell Mom we named Miss Trish the only lady lion in our pride cuz maybe she would get her feelings hurt.

    Love,
    Your frend, Luke

Something to Think About: Sunshine Sits on Dark Days

The little boy turned his attention away from the airplane's window and asked his mother, "Why is the sun always shining up here even when it's dark and cloudy on the ground?"

"The sunshine is always on top, even on dark days," she answered. "Sometimes we have to wait for God to blow the clouds away so it can shine down on us. Other times we have to rise above the dark clouds to see it."

The sun shines on the dark and cloudy days of chronic illness too. While we're experiencing the foggy, shadowy days of hospitals, doctor's offices, and confinement at home, we have three choices.

Choice #1: Rise Above the Clouds

We can choose to see our situation in sunshine's bright and optimistic light. We can smile more and complain less. We can nurture hopeful and healing thoughts instead of dwelling on the negatives. A positive attitude doesn't make the disease go away. It doesn't make the pain any less intense. It is simply a way of rising above the clouds to see the sunshine.

Verbal affirmations are effective for many. Others like to write down inspiring words. Either way, this affirms what's left of our health as well as our faith in God, our family, friends, and church support. It's a wonderful way of reminding us that we possess myriad positives in life.

Rising above the clouds is a gift we can choose to open. Care receivers and caregivers both benefit from standing in the sun's warming rays.

Choice #2: Wait for God to blow the clouds away.

Waiting for God can change your perspective from an inward direction to an outwardly focused one. It requires looking for tiny slivers of sunlight breaking through the dark skies.

Sometimes light shines through people's actions and words. A TV commercial can speak to the heart and give encouragement.

Acts of nature happening outside the window can bring hope. But we have to watch for it.

Choice #3: Be angry, bitter, hostile, and become a person everyone avoids.

This is an option everyone has, whether sick or well. Usually the choice is first made involuntarily. But with practice, it becomes a habit.

To avoid this trip, try reading the psalmist's words:

God, my God, how great you are! beautifully, gloriously robed, dressed up in sunshine, and all heaven stretched out for your tent. You built your palace on the ocean deeps, made a chariot out of clouds and took off on wind-wings. You commandeered winds as messengers, appointed fire and flame as ambassadors. You set earth on a firm foundation so that nothing can shake it, ever.
—Psalm 104:1–5

CHAPTER THIRTEEN

The Rescue

Following the demise of the Wicked Witch of the West, Dorothy set the lion free and helped put Tin Woodsman and Scarecrow back together.

Remembering the promise from the Wizard of Oz, she and her fellow travelers decided to return to him to have their requests granted: brains for Scarecrow, courage for Lion, a heart for Tin Woodsman, and a trip home for Dorothy.

Dorothy packed food from the witch's cupboard and set the witch's golden cap on her head, unaware of the charm it carried. Then they started for the Emerald City once again.

Damp pillows don't always indicate sad hearts. But someone needs to ask.

> So those who planted their crops in despair will shout hurrahs at the harvest, so those who went off with heavy hearts will come home laughing, with armloads of blessing.
> —Psalm 126:5–6

Louis writes...

Dear Lord,

You have given me such a gift. With Danny being here, it has seemed like Christmas every day. I had no idea he was going to be able to stay this long. When I asked him about it, he said not to worry. He's been on the phone to his wife and girls every night. I guess they must be pretty special. He hasn't said a whole lot about them but every once in a while, if I ask, he talks about them.

His wife, Corinne, knows You pretty well it sounds like. She met Danny when she took her car in to get repaired. Something good can come out of a bad transmission after all. He told me the story of how she dragged him off to church before she would let him kiss her good night. Before he knew what had happened, they were standing in front of the preacher saying their vows.

I feel pretty bad about that. Missed a big milestone for him. Guess I missed a lot. Why did I do that? Am I naturally stubborn, or do I just think my way is always right? I don't know. Maybe I should have gone to church a few more times than I did. Perhaps there is something to this religion thing after all.

Lord, I don't know why in the world You would pay attention to my prayer to make things right with Danny. You've got a lot of other people in the world who pay more attention to You than I ever have. Seems like You'd answer their prayers first.

Maybe it doesn't matter. All I know right now is that since I don't know how many days I have left, each one is precious. You must think I'm a sentimental old fool the way I cry over the least little thing. Not sad things—just things that seem special to me.

Like that telephone commercial I saw on TV the other night. A mom and dad were talking to their son. The son was telling them about a new baby coming. And I cried. Maybe because I missed that milestone for Danny too.

I wish I could do it over again. I guess that's why having him here makes me appreciate the time You have given me. I'd like to find some way to make it up to him. I'll have to think about that.

As I closed my eyes last night, I wondered what heaven is like. So I think I'm making progress. I didn't always believe You were real. But after my prayers about Danny were answered, and after the little guy Luke came back to us, I figure I may as well give up trying to ignore You.

That woman Trisha—she seems to think You're the real thing too.

You're awful good to me, Lord. First my wife, who's put up with me for so long. And the kids, all healthy. And now Danny, waiting on me hand and foot. It's enough to make me cry in my pillow every night. And not because I'm sad. Thanks again.

       Amen.

Trisha writes…

Heavenly Father,

It feels good to have a little energy again. Thanks for the magical potion of medicine the nurse injected me with yesterday—the wonderful cell-building stuff. How amazing that two tiny cubic centimeters of anything could make such a difference.

Steven decided to sign up for orchestra at school. The band director is recruiting kids big enough to play the bass. He shouldn't have any problem. He's nearly as tall as Troy. I'm glad he's joining in some activities. I noticed he hasn't been eager to go to anything after school hours. He always rushes home and helps me do whatever I need.

I know I'll be missing many of his big events this year. I feel terrible about that, but what can I do?

After consulting two other oncologists, I've decided to go ahead with another set of chemo treatments. It will debilitate me more than I'd like, but I'll have a better chance of knocking the cancer totally out. I'm all for doing whatever it takes to put a stop to this…once and for all, I hope.

I love this group of people in the clinic. I never thought I would connect with any of the other patients because usually it means listening to a bunch of sad stories. I don't need sad stories. I have enough of my own to carry around. But this little group of ours has become special to me.

I think it all started when little Luke arrived. I know he is supposed to be in the pediatric unit. Since they were out of space, he came to us and I'm glad. He's a precious child and it has been a big help to the rest of us to keep our minds off our own troubles. Whenever we feel sorry for ourselves, we think about him and what he's facing at such a tender, young age.

Lord, when I get to heaven, I'm going to be first in line at the question-and-answer booth. I want to ask why You allow such things to happen to these little ones. I'm giving You plenty of notice, because I need a real answer, not a cliché. The platitude "Trust Me, I have a plan" isn't going to be enough to satisfy me.

I don't mean to be flippant about this, but this issue causes much pain for many people. Even with me, people say, "What a shame, she's so young."

You know I'd like to live a good while longer, but when I think about it, I've had an absolutely wonderful life. I grew up in a home with parents who loved and cared for me. They took me to church, taught me right from wrong, and told me kindness and thoughtfulness counted for a lot. They supported me when I went to college and nursing school and kissed me on the forehead and wished me well when I married Troy. And twelve years ago, You blessed us with Steven.

Of course I long to see him grow up, get married, and have my grandbabies. I want to sit on the porch swing with Troy and watch them play. I want them to crawl all over my lap and beg for my cookies, and I want to teach them silly songs and hear them laugh long and hard.

But apparently my plan may not match up with Yours. And that's okay. Since I've gotten to know You intimately these past months, I know You love me more than I can ever fathom in this world. The day I had the fever You were there. You occupied every single space in my mind. If You hadn't helped me, I would have burned from the inside out.

So what I'm saying is thanks. For every day, for every minute, for each kiss from my husband and son, for the energy to chew, for the ability to swallow, for cool cloths on my forehead, for medicine to fight this disease, for a chance to think, to receive, to relish, to talk with You, to hear from You, and to survive.

It all moves me to tears.

You are my Father. What a tremendous, life-giving word…Father. And I am Your child…Your Trisha.

I love You, Dad.

Amen.

Luke writes…

Dear Jesus,

Today I figgered out I won't be playing soccer again for a very long time. Maybe not even till next year sometime. It made me sad.

I didn't let Mommy see me cry. I did it in my pillo. She can't hear when I do it there.

The Lion Club at the docters is sorta cool. Especially the missions our lady lion dreams up for Danny and the rest of us. It's fun to think of all this as a game. Cuz most days it's not fun at all. The needles. Being all tired. Throwing up.

Being sick makes my throat feel like I swallowed something heavy and my eyes burn until I finally let go and cry.

Then I feel a little better and can fall asleep.

But my pillo gets soggy.

I still love You anyway. I know You're doing the best You know how to do.

Luke

Something to Think About: Soggy Pillows

"I want Sammy to have it." My sister Sue handed my two-year-old a small white pillow with green and yellow flowers on it.

"Are you sure?" I asked. "It's Dougie's pillow...it laid beside him all the time. Don't you want to keep it?"

I wondered how my sister could give up such a meaningful treasure. It was only a few days after the funeral. After Sue lost her only son to cancer at the tender age of two, I couldn't imagine how she could find the strength to give anything away.

"No, Sammy should have it," she replied. "They were the same age. He should have something of Dougie's. The pillow seems right."

My little Sammy, sensing the significance of the moment in his young mind, received the pillow with both hands and clutched it to his chest. It stayed with him day and night through the following week and rode home with him on the airplane. He slept with it every night through the following years. Many evenings, instead of reading a story, he would ask me to "tell the story of Dougie's pillow."

So I would recount the tale of his beloved cousin and the bravery he showed as he endured treatment for a disease with no cure. I spoke of the bravery of his parents and their unending hope for an effective treatment...and of course, a miracle.

Sammy and I tried to imagine what the pillow would say if it could talk. Because soggy pillows talk. They listen well too. Voices too tired to speak to people will talk to pillows. Hands too tired to wipe wet cheeks will let pillows do it for them. Eyes burning with unshed sorrow will blink against the soft covering of a pillow, and the pillow will encourage the tears to come. A head, heavy with thoughts, will find comfort as a pillow receives its weight, molding, fondling, and accepting the head as a gift. A heart, heavy with emotion, when encountering a pillow, will feel lighter having shed its burden of tears into its softness.

The simple comfort of a pillow is one of God's gifts. The simple act of crying is also His gift. Sometimes we cry because of sadness.

Sometimes we cry because of joy. Sometimes we cry because there is nothing else we can do.

> Are you tired? Worn out? Burned out on religion? Come to me. Get away with me and you'll recover your life. I'll show you how to take a real rest. Walk with me and work with me—watch how I do it. Learn the unforced rhythms of grace. I won't lay anything heavy or ill-fitting on you. Keep company with me and you'll learn to live freely and lightly.
> —Matthew 11:28–30

It's okay to cry. Because soggy pillows do talk.
Have you checked the pillows in your house lately?

CHAPTER FOURTEEN

The Winged Monkeys

The travelers resumed their journey, uncertain of the path to take. After a time, they grew discouraged, but they kept walking, thinking they would surely come to someplace soon.

Dorothy asked the field mice for help. They suggested she use the charm of the golden cap to call the winged monkeys to take them to the city of Oz. She followed their advice and learned the story behind the golden cap as the monkeys carried them to the city gate.

Even if you take away a lion's mane, the lion is still a lion.

His huge outstretched arms protect you—under them you're perfectly safe; his arms fend off all harm. Fear nothing—not wild wolves in the night, not flying arrows in the day, not disease that prowls through the darkness, not disaster that erupts at high noon.

—Psalm 91:4–6

Louis writes...

Dear Lord,

Seems like I can't call You anything but Lord. All the other names I've heard for You seem too formal. And after all we've talked about, I think "Lord" suits our relationship.

I've come to the conclusion You really are my Lord. I know it's because of You I've gotten this far. Because of You I have Danny back. Because of You Jan has stuck it out with me. I'm not getting any easier to live with...and now I'm not much to look at either. I'm as bald as a cue ball.

I wasn't sure how I'd feel about not having hair. I almost didn't notice the hair leaving my head because I've been wearing my Yankees cap every day. Then yesterday Danny and I were going to go pick up some medicine and a few things for Jan, and I couldn't find my cap. Danny dug around in the closet and came up with my old fishing hat.

"Here, Dad," he said, "Wear this."

"Let me see that." I took the hat from him. "Boy, this brings back some pleasant memories...entire days floating on the lake...fishing with you and your brothers. There was more floating than fishing as I recall, but it was still good fun."

"I remember. Did you fish much after I left?"

"Some. Not a lot." I smoothed the hat's brim with my fingers. "We need to do that again. Think we can go out on the lake while you're here?"

"I don't see why not. I'll ask around to find out where we could get a boat."

After that conversation, I sort of forgot about my bald head. I concentrated on resting and trying to eat to get some strength back into me, so we could make plans to get out on the water real soon. I figure Danny doesn't have a whole lot of time left to spend with me. I probably don't have much either.

We still have some ground to cover, and I am bound and determined that this time I will not let him leave without saying what needs to be said. I can talk to Michael and JoEllen after he leaves. I should have enough time left.

I will have enough time left, won't I, Lord?

Trisha writes…

Lord Jesus,

I look like a naked, starving chicken. No feathers anywhere. I look in the mirror and see the ugliest person I've ever seen. It's almost as if I'm not a real person anymore. My skin barely covers my bones.

Yesterday, Troy came in the bathroom to help me out of the tub. I happened to glance at my reflection in the mirror as I stepped over the side and I burst into tears!

"What's the matter?" he asked. "Are you hurting?"

"No. Look at me." I barely managed to blubber out the words as I pointed a bony finger at the person in the mirror. "U-u-ugly."

"No way, honey. No way." Troy pulled me close, covering my shivering body with his arms. "Your skin just changed its clothes for a while, that's all. You're still the same beautiful person you always were."

I looked into his concerned, loving eyes. "And you're a sweet, lovable liar." Glancing back at my reflection, I wrapped a towel around me, grabbed a tissue, and blew my nose.

As Troy helped me finish dressing, I was forced to ask myself some tough questions. How did this happen? When had it gotten so bad? What I saw in the mirror looked a lot like pictures I've seen of concentration camp victims in World War II.

I remembered losing the first hair. It didn't seem as traumatic as others had led me to believe. In fact, I enjoyed trying on various styles and colors of wigs. Marcy from church went with me that day. She made the whole thing seem like an exciting adventure. I felt as if I were getting a makeover instead of covering up hair loss. We went out for lunch afterward to celebrate the event. I enjoyed that day tremendously. Bless Marcy for me, will You, Lord?

But when the eyelashes and eyebrows left me, as well as the hair on my arms and legs, the cancer suddenly became real. This would be a fight. I just hadn't realized how battle-scarred I looked until yesterday.

It's not good, is it, Lord?

You don't have to say anything. I have eyes.

Please stay close. My family...and others...will need to see You, and they need to hear Your voice.

As always, I am Your child.

      Trisha

Luke writes...

Dear Jesus,

All my hair came out of my head. I don't have any bristles or anything up there. I look funny.

And I am not the only one. Miss Trish has no hair either. She wears a hat with a flower on it or fake hair to cover up her head. She let me touch her fake hair...it felt real to me. But I also saw her head with nothing on it. She looks okay like that too. I think it's cuz she smiles a lot. When she smiles, I don't notice anything but her smile cuz it covers up her whole face.

I guess I need to smile more. I'm practicing.

Old Louis Lion always looks the same. He's missing hair, too, but you don't notice it cuz of his Yankees cap. He always wears the cap even when he sleeps here. Miss Trish takes her hair off when she sleeps. She says her head likes to breeth. That sounds right to me.

Maybe I should tell the Lions we need to go on a mission to get hair. I wonder where we could look. Miss Trish probably knows since her fake hair looks pretty real.

Old Louis Lion didn't bring his son Danny Lion today. He said he was out looking for a boat. Too bad. I was hoping we could have a comic-book mission again. Maybe tomorrow.

All for now, Jesus. Say hi to the angels from me.
Your frend, Luke

Something to Think About: Outside Coverings

"Mom, I can't find anything to wear!" As teenagers, we all shouted this at least once or twice. Clothes seem to be more than a necessity at that stage of life. They elicit responses of belonging, of beauty, of self-worth. As our tender psyches develop, we look to outside coverings such as clothes to add to our self-esteem.

When chronic disease brings about dramatic changes in appearance, it also removes the security we feel in our own skin. The body in which we had become comfortable leaves us, and it is replaced by one we don't recognize, one we don't want to claim as ours.

For a while, I was able to fool myself. I looked pretty good. I felt halfway decent. My clothes fit better than ever. In fact, I could wear a pair of jeans I hadn't been able to put on for years because they were too tight. I had a wig I loved, which everyone said looked wonderful.

But one bright, revealing day, I saw myself as others were seeing me—emaciated, frail, pale, clothes hanging loosely. It was an awakening. I was really sick. I could die. These were not frenzied thoughts of heaven during a fever. This was not the result of a frantic diet plan to lose weight. This was me, facing the reality of my own death.

It stopped me cold. For about five seconds.

Then into my head popped Scripture verses I had learned as a child...all about heaven, eternity, and the love of a God who gave up everything He had...not for a vague concept like the "entire world," but for me—this emaciated, frail, pale person. He did it for me.

With a reassured heart, the conceitedness of my human nature kicked in quickly, and I once again distracted myself with details such as what to eat, what to drink, and what to wear as I continued on with the business of surviving.

> If you decide for God, living a life of God-worship, it follows that you don't fuss about what's on the table at mealtimes or whether the clothes in your closet are in fashion. There is far more to your life than the food you put in your stomach, more

The Winged Monkeys

> to your outer appearance than the clothes you hang on your body. Look at the birds, free and unfettered, not tied down to a job description, careless in the care of God. And you count far more to him than birds. ...
> What I'm trying to do here is to get you to relax, to not be so preoccupied with getting, so you can respond to God's giving. ...Give your entire attention to what God is doing right now, and don't get worked up about what may or may not happen tomorrow. God will help you deal with whatever hard things come up when the time comes.
> —Matthew 6:25–26, 31, 34

Imagine what the Lord could do if we gave Him all the time we spent hiding evidence of the disease from others. Imagine what He could do if we allowed ourselves to talk about Him as much as we talk about wigs and hats. Just imagine.

Why do words about God and love and family get stuck in our throats, while words about clothes and food and hair come gushing out unchecked?

Maybe it's time to do more than just think about it.

CHAPTER FIFTEEN

The Discovery of Oz the Terrible

The travelers met the Guardian of the Gates and told him the good news about the wicked witch dying. They were allowed to enter the city and the throne room of the great wizard.

But when they asked for heir gifts, the wizard told them they would not be granted their wishes because he had only been "making believe." It turned out the awesome and powerful wizard was only a little man and he had no special powers.

Scarecrow was upset and called the wizard a humbug. The man humbly apologized and said he would do his best to grant their wishes after all. In return, he requested the travelers keep the secret that he was a humbug.

Dorothy hoped Kansas would soon become a reality and she resolved to forgive the fake wizard for his deception…if she ever returned home.

When God gives a promise to mankind, man can ride it all the way to heaven. When man gives a promise to God, it's unusual for anyone to travel anywhere…unless God rides along.

> We were also given absolutely terrific promises to pass on to you—your tickets to participation in the life of God after you turned your back on a world corrupted by lust.
> —2 Peter 1:4

Louis writes...

Dear Lord,

I promised Danny I'd be ready for him this morning. Boy, it's early. The sun's not up yet. Danny's got this crazy idea about seeing the sunrise from the boat.

I guess he rented us a little motor boat for the day. Jan said he spent yesterday scurrying around digging the ice chest out of the basement, figuring out food and drinks to take along, and finding the fishing poles.

I can't imagine him going to all this bother for me. I'd have been happy to take a little row boat out about fifty feet from shore, sit there for an hour, and then row back.

This almost makes me nervous. We've never been together...by ourselves...for a whole day. I wonder what he expects from me. I hope I can handle it.

Guess I'd better stop until later. He's pulling in the driveway. Keep my body strong today, Lord.
                Amen.

What a day! Danny paid a high-school kid to have the boat in the water ready to go when we drove up to the dock. Ice chest and everything was already loaded. I got out of the car, walked about ten steps, and stepped into the boat. Nothing fancy, but it had cushions on the seats and a stadium chair for me to use so my back wouldn't act up.

As I settled into the seat, he pushed us away from the dock, started up the motor, and away we went. We motored out a ways, then he cut the engine and we drifted. No car noise, no people noise, only a few early bird calls and the creaking of the boat. I had forgotten the sound of peace.

I noticed the horizon get lighter. The sun came up right in front of us—all orange and pink, then the sky turned from dark blue to light blue. We watched it all. And we said nothing to each other for a long time.

Danny broke the silence first. "How long's it been, Dad?"

"Hmm?"

"Since you've watched a sunrise?"

I hated to admit it, but I couldn't remember watching a single one on purpose. I had seen some as I was driving here and there, or while working. But to set apart this time of day to do nothing but see the sun coming over the horizon? I didn't think I'd ever done that. Seventy-plus years old and never watched a sunrise on purpose. Sad.

"Don't really know. But I think I'll remember this one the rest of my life." In my mind, I added the words *"Probably won't have to remember it too long."*

"Me too, Dad. Me too."

Danny started to fidget a bit. He cleared his throat. "God's been good to us...getting us together and all, don't you think?"

What was I hearing? Danny was talking about You, Lord! If I wasn't hanging on, I'd have fallen overboard.

"I guess so, Son." I was nearly speechless and completely out of my comfort zone.

"Maybe we should thank Him for it, tell Him we're grateful. Right now." Danny bent his head down, stared at the boat bottom for a moment, then looked at me.

I tell You, Lord, at that instant, I saw in his eyes the little boy who only wanted to please me. I saw this transparent love, hungering for my approval, for my consent to do what should have been a natural act between a father and a son...and that look cut right through me down to the quick.

The guilt and the grief for the kind of father I should have been got all mixed up with the rush of love I was feeling for him. How could I hold myself together? God help me, I am so sorry for what I've done to this boy.

"That would be fine," I told him as I choked back tears.

He closed his eyes. "Lord God, thanks for the great sunrise You shared with us this morning. And most of all, thanks for Dad, and for giving us this time together." He paused. "We've haven't been the best examples of a father and a son, but we're grateful You have given us another chance at it. I think we're beginning to get the idea now. Thanks again. Amen."

Tears pouring from my eyes, I added, "Amen from me, too, Lord." I wouldn't have minded hugging my son right then, but I was afraid I'd rock the boat too much. I did reach over and pat his leg. He covered my hand with his for a moment, then we both had to dig our hankies from our pockets and blow our noses.

Whew! Amazing how much emotion a simple sunrise can drag out of a man.

We hauled out the poles, put the lines in the water, and sat. Talked about this and that. I heard some more about Corinne and the girls. That was nice.

About lunchtime, we motored in to shore and spread out the food he'd packed in the ice chest on a picnic table. The meal actually tasted like food today…must have been the fresh air.

I started pooping out fast after that and Danny noticed. He suggested one more slow ride around the lake and we headed for home.

He helped me get ready for bed. My fingers didn't want to work on my shirt buttons. When he finished with them, he helped me into bed. Then he took my hands in his and said, "Sleep well. Say your prayers. Thanks for the day. I love you, Daddy."

Daddy! Hadn't called me that since he was a kid.

Lord Almighty, if You want to take me home tonight, I'm ready to go. My son loves me!
      Amen.

Trisha writes…

Heavenly Father,

I've tried to talk to Troy about him getting remarried after I die. He won't listen. He tries to walk away. I told him sooner or later we would all die and that I was trying to get things ready. I wanted to make him promise he would look for someone else. It would be better for Steven to have a mom to help him through these teen years.

But Troy said, "Don't be stupid. You're too young to die. I'm not going to talk about it and that's final."

Lord, I don't know exactly when You plan to take me, but I think I'm going to need to hang around awhile to help Troy get used to the idea of living without me.

Strangely enough, I think Steven will be fine. All those years of bedtime Bible stories are paying off. He knows heaven is the goal of living. Troy knows, too, although for some reason, he thinks if he doesn't talk about it, it won't happen.

I know the doctor said everything's going fairly well, but I have this feeling. So please give me the chance to talk some sense into Troy. I'd even like a chance to plan my own funeral…and it would be good if we could do it together.

I'm really tired today, Father. And I've got another round of chemo to face in the morning. Hold me awhile, please?
                Amen.

Luke writes…

Dear Jesus,

I am liking this pride of Lions a whole lot. I think the docter thinks its pretty cool too. Miss Trish keeps coming up with these crazy missions for Danny Lion. Today she gave him a envalope with a message inside that said to go find us some happy hats. Whoever heard of that! I guess she has. It made me laugh and Old Lion Louis laughed too.

So Danny Lion left and didn't come back for a long time. When he got back he had a really big sack with him and he had this pink hat with two smashed-up yellow flowers on it and a hole on each side, and he put it on his head and said, "This happy hat's mine because it makes me laugh when I wear it. You other Lions will have to fight over the rest of the hats."

I asked him where he got the pink hat with the smashed yellow flowers and holes, and he said it came from Bluebell, the horse that pulls the buggy in the park! He said she wasn't too happy about him taking it, but he told her it was for the Lions in the building across the street, and I guess the horse didn't want to tangle with us Lions cuz we're scary! How funny this whole thing is.

The other hats were all crazy. I got a red one with two big eyes on it. Miss Trish wanted the purple floppy one that hides her face and Old Louis got one with a fish with a mouth that opens and shuts.

Miss Trish was a little tired today and she didn't wear her happy hat very long. Maybe you could help her sleep better tonight.

Guess I better be getting to bed too. Night, Jesus!
I love You! Amen.

                Love,
                Luke

Something to Think About: Happy Hats

Somewhere along the journey of chronic illness, the sick person may choose to put on a happy hat. The happy hat comes out whenever company visits or when family members and caregivers express doubt, anger, or impatience with the current state of affairs. Because the sufferer is not always able to lend a hand with the household activities, the person may feel that wearing the happy hat is the only contribution he or she can make.

Sometimes the happy hat becomes glued to the head and no one is allowed to see how the sick person looks without it. After a time, it becomes as heavy as a knight's helmet, pressing down on the scalp until raging headaches develop. The sick person may actually gain weight from taking on loads of guilt and anguish. The happy smile, frozen in place, does not unthaw and slide off the face until nightfall covers it safely under the pillow of darkness.

The happy hat can become a source of contention between the sick person and the caregiver. When the doorbell rings, the happy hat is swished from the bedside table and placed on the head. The smile is glowing and charming. The mouth moves, the right words float through the room. But as soon as the door closes behind the visitor, the happy hat is flung across the room to the farthest dark corner. The sick person becomes the sneering troll under the bridge, lying in wait to ambush the caregiver at the first opportunity.

Being sick day after day after day presents a challenge like no other. Through trial after trial, test after test, hope is attacked, buoyed, and then annihilated. Promise after promise is presented on the silver platters of prescription pads and magical infusions.

It's like waiting for a Christmas that never comes. When there are no more presents to unwrap, when the magic has been depleted, both sufferer and caregiver can come to a transforming awareness. The transformation occurs when they open the Book and read together:

> Even when the way goes through Death Valley, I'm not afraid when you walk at my side. Your trusty shepherd's crook makes me feel secure. You serve me a six-course dinner right in front of

my enemies. You revive my drooping head; my cup brims with blessing. Your beauty and love chase after me every day of my life. I'm back home in the house of God for the rest of my life.
—Psalm 23:4–6

CHAPTER SIXTEEN

The Magic Art of the Great Humbug

One at a time, the travelers approached the wizard to receive their requests. The scarecrow's head was removed and stuffed with a mixture of bran, pins, and needles. The wizard said he had given him "bran-new brains." Then he cut a hole in the tin woodsman's chest and placed a stuffed silk heart inside. The lion drank a liquid from a green-gold dish. The wizard called it Liquid Courage.

The three travelers were happy because they imagined the wizard could do anything.

Dorothy's wish proved to be more difficult. The wizard needed a few days to think about it. He knew it would take more than imagination to carry Dorothy back to Kansas. And he wasn't sure how he could do it.

As our heavenly Father, God doesn't make any mistakes. As His kids, we can count on Him fixing anything we mess up.

God means what he says. What he says goes. His powerful Word is sharp as a surgeon's scalpel, cutting through everything, whether doubt or defense, laying us open to listen and obey. Nothing and no one is impervious to God's Word. We can't get away from it—no matter what.

—Hebrews 4:12–13

Louis writes…

Dear Lord,

I never dreamed that at my age I would feel as carefree and downright happy as I am right now. All it took was for Danny to come home. How did You know that? Why did You decide to make it happen now? It's almost scary to think about.

With the excitement of him being here—taking me to chemo and spending time going places—I've neglected Michael and JoEllen. I'm sorry. I sure don't want anything standing between any of us.

I told JoEllen last Saturday night when she came by that I was proud of her. Should have told her long ago. She started crying and said, "Dad, are you feeling okay?"

What a mess I must have been, Lord! For my only daughter to wonder if something was wrong with me when I gave her a compliment. How did You tolerate my stubbornness and insensitivity for so long? And how has Jan managed to keep her sanity and to love me all these years? She must be one of Your special people they call saints. Maybe all these years she's been praying for You to change me or even to take me to heaven. I don't know.

After seeing the turnaround with Danny, I know I don't need to worry about JoEllen. She's happy. She's doing her thing. She has friends. She has church. And bless her, she doesn't need a husband. I'm going to stop bugging her about it. It's a new concept for me, to think that not every woman needs a man.

I've got to talk to Michael before too much more time goes by. He's always played it pretty straight, doing the right thing, making the right choices, except for the speeding tickets thing. But I guess he had to sow his oats somehow. JoEllen would say I'm prejudiced if she heard me say that about Michael, and maybe I am. Just a little, though. I'm learning.

Now, about this cancer thing, Lord. (Do You know that's the first time I've said the actual word? I guess You do.) I've always looked at it as a huge pain in the b-u-double-t, excuse my language. But I'm not seeing it like that anymore. Look at the great things that have happened because of it. My changed attitude toward You. My new outlook on church. My improved relationship with Danny. It's not all bad.

I never believed all those "God is working everything together for good" verses in the Bible...until now. Now I think You really meant it. Every word. What a thing to find out at my age.

I'd like to be bold and ask You to let me hang around a bit longer. I know I don't deserve to, but last Sunday at church, I heard the preacher say we have all sinned. We can't earn our way into heaven. That's why You sent Your Son, Jesus, to live and die for us. I can't begin to conceive of why You did that, Lord. I could never give up Danny for anyone, especially a bunch of strangers.

But I did give up Danny when I let him go flying out the door all those years ago. I was wrong. I shouldn't have blown up. I should have listened.

Now I want some time with him. Is that so awful? Is it asking too much?

If I understand what the Bible says correctly, You want us all to be together in heaven one day. I wonder...will it really last forever?

Lord, please, take this cancer away! I *need* another chance. Danny loves You. Maybe he can teach me how to love You more. I don't think I'm too old to learn.

Thanks for listening. I hope You had time to hear me.
     Amen.

Trisha writes...

Dear Lord,

Something's wrong. We were having a perfectly normal day in the clinic, verging on the point of actual fun, when Doc came in, pulled up a chair, and sat beside me.

"Trisha," he said, "I'd like to run a few more tests. Your counts haven't responded as well as I'd like. How about tomorrow?"

I'm not stupid. I've seen too many doctors deliver too many bad tidings to patients over the years.

"I was coming here anyway for the usual stuff. So I guess whatever you think is appropriate will be okay with me." I am sick of asking, *"What tests?"* and, *"For what purpose?"* and, *"What are the side effects?"* and, *"How will it help or guide my treatment?"*

"Great," Doc said. "I'll see you tomorrow then. Don't eat or drink anything after midnight. You know the drill." Then he left.

Oh, I know the drill, all right. I've been drilling patients probably longer than he's been alive, but of course I couldn't tell him that. It wouldn't be polite. And if there's one thing I am, it's polite. It's like a curse. My mom and dad ingrained it deeply in my character. I wonder if Steven will be the same way.

Speaking of Mom and Dad, I guess it's time to update them again. I hate doing it. They've lived mostly in a generation that thinks of cancer as a terminal disease, fatal all the time. I keep telling them it's *chronic*. With the modern advances in medicine and technology, the doctors can probably keep me alive for years, still carrying a diagnosis of cancer.

But Mom and Dad love me, so they worry. I guess I'd be doing the same thing if it were Steven.

I'm not sure if I should tell Troy and Steven that the doctor wants to take more tests. Maybe it'd be better to wait and tell them after the results come back. That would buy me another three days or so.

I don't have a clue what's going on, but I know You're in charge. I need to be here for this little guy named Luke and also for crusty old "Louis Lion," as Luke calls him. His son, Danny, is certainly bringing Luke out of his shell. I'll have to come up with another "Lion Mission" for tomorrow when I'm not here. They need something to keep them going. As honorary Lioness, I want to live up to my title.

Maybe Steven can give me an idea when I get home this afternoon.

Talk to You later, Lord.
                    Amen.

Luke writes...

Hi, Jesus!

I feel great today. Miss Trish told Danny Lion he had his werk cut out for him. He asked Miss Trish why he always had to do the missions. She told him as the only lion in the pride who had a father here, it was his job to make his dad proud and to keep our pride on the rite track. I think old Louis Lion liked that, cuz he and Danny smiled a lot at each other, and at us too.

Miss Trish told Danny Lion his mission for the day was to scour the area for real bone-a-fide circus peanuts, whatever that is. She said all lions should have the experience of biting into a circus peanut, even if they aren't in the circus.

She told Danny the circus peanuts had to be orange and soft, and there must be a whole bagful so every lion in the pride would get to have a lot of them. "Good luck," she said, "and may the force of Lions everywhere be with you."

He laughed and said he would do his best. I wondered where in the world he would find circus peanuts. I didn't think there were any circuses around here.

But after a while he came back holding a sack. He said to me, "Close your eyes and open your mouth."

I did. Next thing I know, something's in my mouth, and he says, "Take a bite." I did and *wow!* If that's what circus peanuts taste like, I think I want to be a real lion and join the circus, or at least feed the lions so I can sneek some now and then.

I opened my eyes and saw they really were orange. And they tasted so sweet! And everybody was happy and smiling. I wish I could feel this good forever. I'm almost feeling good enuf to run again.

Thank You, Jesus, for this great day. And for helping the medisin to keep werking rite.
                        Amen.
                        Love,
                        Luke

Something to Think About: Tests

I stood on the rim of the Grand Canyon. Its beauty beckoned, pulling me forward like the call of the sirens drew Ulysses. I wanted to explore its depths, to begin the journey down into its crevices, but the guide told me it couldn't be done in an hour or two. It would take time. If I signed up for an overnight trip, I needed to go back to the hotel and put on proper shoes and clothing. I wondered if I was strong enough to make the excursion.

"We need more tests."

Hearing this statement feels like standing on the rim of the Grand Canyon. The beauty of knowledge calls out to us. It would be good to know what the aches mean, where the pain originates. It would be good to know the reason for the cough, for the fatigue. Wouldn't it?

Testing constitutes the first step of the journey into the canyon. But it promises nothing. No answers. No guarantees. So why sign the consent forms? Why endure the agonies of such rigorous travel?

Because the knowledge may reveal a spectacular sunrise...a sunrise whose bright rays expose answers and hope. And for hope we ignore the blisters on our feet and the pain in our lower backs, and we continue the journey forward in spite of the uncertain destination. We cling to a guide who always knows the way, who shows us the path, who holds the world in the palm of His hand.

> God, the one and only—I'll wait as long as he says. Everything I hope for comes from him, so why not? He's solid rock under my feet, breathing room for my soul, an impregnable castle: I'm set for life. My help and glory are in God—granite-strength and safe-harbor-God—so trust him absolutely, people; lay your lives on the line for him. God is a safe place to be.
> —Psalm 62:5–8

If you reach the canyon floor and hear, "I'm sorry. We don't know the way out of here," it is time to ask the guide's name. If the response is not "God," it's time to find Him.

He is solid rock. He is breathing room. He is impregnable. You can trust Him absolutely.

CHAPTER SEVENTEEN

How the Balloon Was Launched

The Wizard of Oz finally sent for Dorothy and told her of a possible way to return to Kansas. He would make a hot-air balloon that would carry her all the way home. She agreed and he constructed a balloon.

He decided to come with her, as he was from Omaha. As he waited inside the balloon's basket for her to grab her little dog, Toto, and climb in with him, the balloon's ropes snapped and it took off without her. That was the last anyone saw of the Wizard of Oz. Everyone hoped he made it safely to Omaha.

No paths exist in the sands of the desert. Instead, the sun shines.

> But he brought his people out like a flock; he led them like sheep through the desert. He guided them safely, so they were unafraid; but the sea engulfed their enemies.
> —Psalm 78:52–53 NIV

Louis writes…

Dear Lord,
    Candy circus peanuts! How does she do it? Dreaming up such silly things for Danny to fetch? Miss Trish sure keeps

things lively around here. I wonder what crazy thing she will ask him to find today.

Doc came in yesterday. Talked to all of us a minute or two, but I noticed he spent more time with Miss Trish. Sounds as if she has to go through some more testing. Hope it turns out okay for her.

Our Little Lion Luke is getting stronger by the day. It helps pass the time for him when he's distracted with us grown-ups behaving like a bunch of kids. I have to say it helps pass the time for me too.

I can't believe Danny insisted on wearing the pink hat with flowers this morning. He put it on as soon as we got out of the car in the parking garage and left it on all the way into the building and as we rode up the elevators. I don't mind playing along for the kid in the clinic room, but that guy in the suit in the elevator gave Danny a look You wouldn't believe. And of course the receptionist and nurses in the office and the other people waiting to see the doc all hooted and howled like crazy as we sat down.

It was good to hear the waiting room fill up with laughter and replace the painful silence that usually lives there. Danny just grinned. He must get the silly streak from Jan's side of the family.

We got settled into our recliners. Me, the guy in overalls, and the kid, and Danny in Miss Trish's chair. She's not here yet. Overalls tells me today is his last treatment. He's been cleared for takeoff. Good for him. One day it might be me saying those words. He doesn't like to play games, though. Spends his time reading the paper and then takes a nap, which is okay with me. I don't think he would make a good Lion for our pride.

Listen to me. A grown man pretending he's a lion! Oh, well, like I said—it passes the time.

Here she comes, our Lioness, with that big red bag slung over her shoulder. We're in trouble now. Or rather, Danny's in trouble for sitting in her chair.

"Danny Lion!" She stood in front of him, plopped down her bag, and put her hands on her hips. "Get that hat off your head, get out of my chair, and get ready for your mission of the day."

Danny jumped to attention. It's a riot, watching these two go at it. Luke's grinning like a little clown.

"Yes, Madame Lioness, I am here to do your bidding." Danny bowed low.

Where did he learn to talk like that? He must have read stories to his girls.

"We lions have soft pads on our feet and a big forest to walk through. We will need extra protection for our journey, because sometimes the path is thorny. You have heard of the lion with the thorn stuck in his paw, haven't you?"

"Yes, Madame Lioness, I know the story well." Danny bowed again.

Luke leaned forward, eager to hear the mission.

"Sometimes the path is rocky and cold as well. We are special lions so we must have special coverings for our feet. So we will need, each of us, warm and cozy socks with toes in them. Each sock must have five places for our toes to fit into. And it wouldn't hurt if each of the toes were brightly colored. It will make our journey less boring if we can look down and see pretty colors on our feet."

She handed Danny an envelope. She leaned close and whispered to him that she'd put some money inside to get the job done and included instructions about where to find the special socks. Good thing! I could see by the look on Danny's face he didn't have the slightest idea where to look for socks with toes in them. He probably didn't know there was such a thing. Neither did I.

But off he went, with the envelope and a great big smile.

So now it's time to settle down and get these intravenous bags running. Miss Trish took a squeeze ball out of her bag and gave it to Luke to use when they start him up. Then she settled back in her chair and closed her eyes like she was out of energy.

She doesn't look so great today. Funny how I expect her to always be lively...but I guess everyone has a down day now and then. I'll try to keep Luke occupied so she can rest today.

Talk to you later, Lord. Thanks for this time, this medicine, the people here, and my family.
    Amen.

Trisha writes...

Lord, I am so tired. Testing day has arrived. Getting here took more out of me than I figured it would. Maybe because I haven't eaten. The nurse said they were almost ready for me upstairs. Let the games begin.

I wish I weren't a nurse. I wish I didn't know the things I know. It would buy me a few more days of blissful ignorance.

Here comes the nurse. Guess it's time to go. I hope I get back in time to see if Danny Lion finds the socks. He's a good person to play along with the story. It really helps Luke.

I'm going to call Mom and Dad tonight. It's time they knew things are changing. It will be good to hear their voices.

More later, Lord. I'm sure we'll be talking soon after these tests. Stay close, okay?
    Amen.

Luke writes...

Dear Jesus,

I didn't know you made socks with toes! I can't wait for Danny Lion to come back from his mission so I can see what they look like. My socks at home are all black or white. Well, some of the white ones are gray now from when I went outside without my shoes on.

How the Balloon Was Launched

I bet the socks with colored toes that Danny Lion went to find will be funny. Maybe they will make each toe feel so good that they will get stronger and I will be able to run faster than ever. Maybe pretty soon I can play soccer again.

Miss Trish gave me a ball to squeeze today. It's blue and green and looks like the world. When I hold it in my hand I wonder if You feel like this when You hold the real world in Your hand. Is our world heavy or lite? Can you feel all of us peeple walking around in it? Does it seem like ants are crawling in Your hand?

I'm really happy You don't squeeze us.

Pleese help Danny Lion find the socks fast. My toes are wondering what they will feel like.

                Amen.
                Your friend,
                Luke

Something to Think About: Distractions

Circus peanuts, socks with toes, pink hats, silly people. All are distractions in the desert. It doesn't make the trip across the hot sand any less real, but it makes it more bearable. This trek remains an arduous, exhausting walk over miles and miles of sand that is continually shifting, moving, and blowing in the traveler's face.

I wonder...Do other chemotherapy rooms have people in them who bring circus peanuts and squeeze balls?

I really did buy squeeze balls. A fellow patient named Mrs. Middlebrooks brought the circus peanuts. When she first pulled the candy out of her bag, I thought, *How can she eat those? They're so unhealthy for us.*

But as Mrs. Middlebrooks shared her candy, I listened to her stories about when she was a girl and how much she loved circus peanuts. I could see that they gave her much more than a sugar rush. For Mrs. Middlebrooks they represented a step back in time, a memory of happier days, an excuse to share herself with fellow travelers.

For the rest of us, each distraction served as an oasis in the desert. It offered cool, refreshing waters that helped wash away the heat of the day. It gave our minds the gift of forgetfulness. We travelers welcomed each opportunity to forget that we were traveling on a journey for which we didn't buy a ticket.

Laughing and teasing and make-believe may seem inappropriate while fighting the battle for life, but they are tension-relieving treasures. It is possible to experience joy in the middle of a desert storm.

> Be joyful always; pray continually; give thanks in all circumstances, for this is God's will for you in Christ Jesus.
> —1 Thessalonians 5:16–18 NIV

Here's how *The Message* translates that verse:

> Be cheerful no matter what; pray all the time; thank God no matter what happens. This is the way God wants you who belong to Christ Jesus to live.

How the Balloon Was Launched

So bring the circus peanuts. Or the socks with toes in them. Or the squeeze balls. Or the pink hat with yellow flowers. Or laughter. But bring something...because someone will always be looking for an oasis in the desert.

And pick up a pair of X-ray vision glasses while you're at it. They may give you insight into choosing the appropriate time for sharing the distractions.

CHAPTER EIGHTEEN

Away to the South

The travelers were sorry at losing the wizard, but three of them were grateful and content with his gifts to them. Still, they thought it sad that Dorothy was not able to return home.

A soldier with green whiskers advised them to seek the help of Glinda, the Good Witch of the South. Because the road to the south held many dangers, the tin woodsman, the scarecrow, and the lion all decided to accompany Dorothy on the journey to help her. They would leave in the morning.

When endurance becomes weariness, and encouragement evaporates, call on God. It wouldn't hurt to call in the cavalry as well, especially if they are riding for Him.

> May our dependably steady and warmly personal God develop maturity in you so that you get along with each other as well as Jesus gets along with us all. Then we'll be a choir—not our voices only, but our very lives singing in harmony in a stunning anthem to the God and Father of our Master Jesus!
> —Romans 15:5–6

Louis writes…

Dear Lord,

Here we are again…another crazy day in chemo-land. I could not believe the goofy socks Danny came back with yesterday. There really are socks with toes in them, sort of like gloves for your feet. And all the toe places were wacky colors like hot pink, purple, and green.

Little Luke laughed long and loud as he promptly whipped off his socks and shoes and put the new socks on his feet. Then he held up the other pairs Danny had bought and said the rest of us lions had to put our socks on too.

I really didn't want to do the socks. I kind of thought we should call a halt to this silliness somewhere, and this seemed like a good place to start. But he and Danny insisted, and I couldn't turn both of them down. Unfortunately, they make these crazy socks in all sizes. So off went my boring black argyles and on went the clown socks.

I'm for sure going to take them off before we get in the elevator.

Miss Trish had a rough day yesterday. She didn't get to start her treatment until after she finished the other test upstairs. So she was probably here until suppertime. No wonder she looks beat today. I think Luke and I will toss the squeeze ball around with Danny and let her sleep. I wonder why her husband and son never come with her. I guess maybe they're working and in school.

Jan and I had a good long visit last night after Danny turned in for the night. She's happy about the change in me, and I told her I was sorry for being such a crusty old fool all these years. She just laughed and hugged me around the neck and said I was a cute crusty old fool. I don't know what she sees in me…but I'm glad she does.

Danny has to leave in the next few days. Sure is going to be tough to see him go. I am proud that he had the guts to come and talk to me like he did. I don't know if I could have done it. I'm glad I didn't have to try.

The other Lions will miss him too. He's gotten quite attached to little Luke.

I'd better stop, Lord. I'll talk to You again later today. I'm realizing it doesn't have to be nighttime or mealtime for me to visit with You. What a wonderful thing that is to know.

So amen for now.

Louis

Trisha writes...

Lord God,

I called Mom and Dad last night. Troy wasn't sure I should, because he figured they would jump in the car and head this way as soon as they heard we were waiting for results from another test. It's no small trip for them. A seven-hour ride is a long way these days.

And, of course, they are coming. They should be pulling in the driveway around four this afternoon. I'll be done with chemo by then and back home. I need to think about what we should eat for dinner, but right now, I only want to talk with You.

I need my parents here right now. I can't say exactly why. I think I'd like them to be with me when I get the results from this last test, especially since Troy will be working and Steven will be at school. It's not that I'm expecting bad news, but I'm not expecting good news, either, judging from the doctor's tone of voice.

I must be feeling a little sorry for myself. I have to admit, I'm tired of being alone. There are people all around me, but I still feel alone. I'd like to share, to talk more, especially with the others who come here for treatment, but for some reason I feel as if it's my job to keep their spirits up. Guess that's my nursing brain kicking into gear.

Mom and Dad will be wonderful. They always are. They'll let me talk, or sleep, or be quiet, or whatever. They won't push. And when I need them, they'll be there.

They're simply the best.

Hope they're being careful on the road. I wish four o'clock would hurry up and come. Watch over them, Lord.
Amen.

Luke writes...

Hi, Jesus!

Did you invent those funny socks? If you didn't I would like to meet whoever did. They are the funniest things I have ever had on my feet.

Boy, it's getting hard to sit here and watch this stuff drip through the tubes into me. These grown-ups are nice and kind of funny, but I want to go back to school and be with my friends. Do you spose You could make that happen, Jesus? It's no fun doing werk from school by myself.

Besides, I think I'm breething good now, and I can almost run agin, so I'm probly good enuf to be at my desk, even if I have to stay in for recess. Mom would be happy about it, I think. Curtis mite not be happy if I took my place back on the team.

Oh, well. It should be my turn now anyway.
Amen.
Your friend,
Luke

Something to Think About: The Cavalry

My throat was parched. My lips felt like sandpaper. I slowly opened one eye. A tall glass of water with ice cubes came into my view. How had it gotten there? Oh, yes…the cavalry. How could I have forgotten?

I slowly pushed myself up from the bed on one elbow and drank the entire glass. Much better. I sat up completely and gazed around my bedroom.

I wondered what had happened to the tulips. Yesterday I thought I'd have to throw them out. But today they looked freshly picked. Oh, yes…the cavalry again.

A blanket lay neatly folded across the foot of my bed. It hadn't been there last night. The cavalry must have brought it in while I slept, concerned that I might be cold.

Mom and Dad…my own personal cavalry. They had come to fill in the gaps, to stay with me while the rest of my family tried to resume some semblance of a normal routine. Mom and Dad had always been very good at anticipating my needs. I would barely bring a thought or desire to my mind when they were already carrying it through.

I finally asked them how they knew what I needed so quickly.

They said they simply put themselves in my place, tried to think what I might be feeling, and then figured out what I might need. It was a great system, and I was extremely thankful to receive their love and support in such tangible ways.

Their selfless acts brought to my mind another cavalry. A Person who had put Himself in my place. Who didn't have to try to think of what I might be feeling, but actually knew. I had known the Savior for my entire life, but until the whole "cancer journey," I had never known such a depth of appreciation for the Calvary he endured for me. For that alone, I felt it was worth traveling every step of the journey.

I prayed to be given the chance to be the cavalry for others, so they too would know what He did for them and could encounter Him face to face.

To everyone currently serving as cavalry,

To everyone enjoying the blessings of a cavalry,

To anyone who may be called into active duty as a cavalry soon,

May you all be injected with a new awareness and gratitude of what He did for us on that long weekend, not so very long ago.

Thanks again, Mom and Dad. You're the best!

CHAPTER NINETEEN

Attacked by the Fighting Trees

The travelers headed south and slept on the grass that night, with nothing but the stars over them. They rested well.

The next morning they reached the edge of the forest. Each time Scarecrow tried to pass through the trees, a branch would reach down, grab him, and throw him back. The tin woodsman put a stop to the nonsense by chopping off the attacking branches, thus allowing the travelers to enter the woods.

They continued walking until they were stopped by a high, smooth, white china wall. Tin Woodsman said he knew a way for them to get over it.

When traveling to Oz, upon encountering a wall, only four options exist: climb over it, tunnel beneath it, discover a way around it, or morph through it.

> You'll use the old rubble of past lives to build anew, rebuild the foundations from out of your past. You'll be known as those who can fix anything, restore old ruins, rebuild and renovate, make the community livable again.
> —Isaiah 58:12

Louis writes...

Dear Lord,

Thank You, thank You, thank You! Doc said I will be finished with treatments after this week. I'm all set, I've been cleared, everything looks great. The cough is gone, my blood is good, life is grand.

For a while there, I wondered if You knew what You were doing...I even wondered if You were real. But my whole life has changed because of this. To think it all started with a little cough. Imagine that.

I made a deal with You when we started this mess. I shouldn't have done that. I asked You for more years and said that if You gave them to me, I'd show up at church more and do some work for You. I realize now that it's not about "deals." You have loved me all along even though I behaved exactly like Danny when he ran out on me as a kid. I ran out on You, didn't I? I ignored the help You offered along the way. I figured all I had in this world belonged to me because I had earned it myself, no thanks to anybody else. I believed Jan came to be my wife because I was silver-tongued and handsome. Ha! She is definitely at the top of the list of Your best gifts to me.

And then, I get this cancer and figure my time's about up. Now, You not only spring this surprise reconciliation with Danny on me, but You also take this disease away. I can honestly say that I'd die a happy man if I died tomorrow because my son has forgiven me. Getting to know him has put a whole new spin on things. Getting to know You has put a whole new spin on things too. Can't imagine what held me away from You all these years. My own selfish pride, I suppose.

Anyway, Lord, things will be different now. Help me be smart enough to see the great blessings You have put in my life. Help me be courageous enough to say the hard stuff. To stop swallowing those words that choke me up. Words like "I'm proud of you" and "I love you."

Give me courage like a lion, like the courage You give little Luke and Miss Trish.

Give me courage like You gave Danny when he came to clear things up with me. It's sad I couldn't have done it myself, being the father and all. But I am very thankful You made it happen for me anyhow.

Now it's like starting over again, except from a different place. What do You want me to do? I don't feel it's right to sit and do nothing or to do the same things I've always done because I'm not the same person. I'm asking for some ideas here, Lord. My imagination has gotten a little better since this whole "lion pride" started, but this is real life. I don't want to make stupid mistakes again.

I should have asked for Your help in the first place. But I've learned my lesson and so I'm asking for Your help now. Two more days and I'll be a free man. Freedom, at the tender young age of seventy-one. Takes some people longer than others to learn the taste of freedom. Couldn't have found it without You.

I would appreciate it if You gave me some courage tomorrow. I'm going to have to tell the other Lions I'll be starting another pride of my own.

My stomach has butterflies.
      Amen.

Trisha writes…

Dear Lord of all things and all people,

Waiting is always the most difficult part for me. The tests and procedures seem easy in comparison. I guess because waiting implies sitting and doing nothing. Going no place. Nothing happening. And if nothing is happening, then I'm not getting better.

Not that I think I will get better. But I won't know for sure until tomorrow, when the results come back.

Thanks for bringing Mom and Dad here safely. They're making the best of it, though I can see their concern written all over their faces. It feels so right to have them here. It's good for Troy and Steven too. They don't have to feel pressured to hurry home to help me.

I managed to talk with Troy as we were lying in bed last night. I think he wanted to go to sleep, but I could tell from his breathing he was still awake.

"Troy?"

"Need something, honey?" he mumbled.

"You." I put him in the spoon position, with my front hugging his back.

"I'm here for you, you know that," he said to the wall.

"Yes, you are. For now. I need you to be here for me later too...even if I'm not around."

"I told you to stop talking like that. The tests will come back tomorrow and everything will be fine." He spoke with firmness, as if by being emphatic the words would be true.

"Maybe," I said, "but maybe not. And it's the maybe-not part we need to talk about."

He was quiet. With my arm slung over his chest, I could feel his heart rate increase and his breathing become shallow. I laughed to myself. Always a nurse. Even in the most difficult of circumstances, here I was assessing his physical reaction, planning the next step, trying to intervene.

"Okay," he said softly.

That was my cue. "If...If I die while Steven is in his teens, I want you to pray about finding another wife. If God should bring someone to you, I don't want you to waste time feeling guilty or sad about me. Just go ahead and get married again. I think you and Steven would both be happier." I waited to see if he would respond.

He said nothing. But his heart rate stayed up.

"I've written down some details about my funeral service. Things like the songs to sing and the Bible verses I like best. I want it to be a worship service, not a memorial service. People should be telling God how great He is for giving us this time together. They should walk out of those church doors feeling thankful from the tops of their heads to the tips of their toes, because they can look forward to heaven."

Still no reaction from him. *Let me try another approach.*

"I want an open casket, and I made a sign I want you to place on my chest. It says, 'This is not me. I look a whole lot better now. I've gone to heaven. See you when you get here.'"

He rolled over to face me. His face looked shocked. "You can't be serious."

Finally. A reaction.

"Okay, maybe the sign is overdoing it a little." I couldn't keep myself from chuckling. "But I wish you would put those words someplace where people could read them. Maybe in the worship folder. Folks need to know that dying is a good thing when God's in the middle of it."

He shook his head. "You're crazy, you know that?" He grinned and gave a weak laugh as he cradled my head with his arm.

"I'm only trying to make things easier for you, honey. I want you to welcome the future, even if it's without me." I took his hand in both of mine. "Aren't you the least bit curious?"

"About what?"

"About where I put my funeral details list."

"I don't want to know."

"Guess I'd better tell you now because you may need to get started on it. It'll take some time."

"Time for what?"

"To get everybody lined up."

"What?"

"Singers, dancers, fiddlers. You'll have to wrap gifts, call the caterers, clean the bathrooms, hire a band—"

"You *are* crazy!"

"Just for that, I'm going to make you beg me to tell you where I hid the list!" I laughed and started tickling and tormenting him. "Go on, beg!"

My tickling reduced him to tears. Me too. But they were satisfying tears. Tears of joy and of sorrow. Tears for the past and for the future.

He begged. I still didn't tell him.

Maybe tomorrow I will.

But in case tomorrow on earth never comes for me, the service list is between the mattress and box spring.

On my side of the bed.

See you later, Lord.
    Amen.

Luke writes…

Dear Jesus,

I wore my toe socks today. Good thing, too, cuz Miss Trish didn't have a mission for us lions today.

Can I go back to school soon? Mom says we have to wait for the doctor to say its okay, but I figger You know more and would have the final say-so. I think I'm ready. And since Miss Trish ran out of missions it would be a good time.

Plese think about it.
    Amen and love,
    Luke

Something to Think About: Walls

Walls serve a variety of purposes. Some commemorate—like the Vietnam War memorial. Others contain—as in defense or building a home. Some walls challenge—as in an athletic competition. During chronic illness, walls serve all three purposes.

For the ill person, time is difficult to mark. Days seem endless, nights seem even longer. Nothing sets time apart when a job schedule is not in place. Purpose for living becomes vague as the colors of a meaningful existence run together. Caught up in a society where personal identification centers on a specific job or occupation, the ill person can lose a sense of identity. His or her family may also lose interest in a schedule that centers on mealtimes, bathroom visits, and doctor appointments.

So the wall becomes a marker in the individual's mind, with commemorative dates etched on it: date of the diagnosis, date of the first hospitalization, procedure, or surgery. Everything else seems insignificant.

The wall can also serve as a container for bottling emotions and feelings. Safety exists within a container. If the lid is not removed, there is no danger of anything spilling. For the sufferer, every person walking through the bedroom door presents a potential danger.

Each sympathetic, loving visitor runs the risk of removing the lid from the container and standing in a mess of spilled emotions. Then both sufferer and visitor are faced with a two-fold dilemma: How can we clean up this mess, and how comfortable do we feel standing in these turbulent waters? Many times, the visitor simply looks for the quickest escape route, leaving the sufferer standing alone in the rushing current to eventually be pulled under by the riptide.

Finally, the ill person may see the wall as an obstacle. A plate of food may represent the wall. Each bite can seem as impossible to swallow as swimming the English Channel. A trip to the bathroom may be a wall. The first walk down a corridor without assistance. Going to a church service during a period of remission. Sharing test results with the family.

For me, the obstacle was an actual wall. I was given a video with daily exercises to follow. The exercises were supposed to restore my arm to full range of motion following the surgery. The position to assume was against a wall. I chose the wall beside my bed, in case I needed to sit or lie down.

I began the exercises with a holier-than-thou attitude. I viewed the video first, pooh-poohing them as too simplistic. After all, in my pre-cancer life, I was a rigorous exerciser, both at the gym and at home. But someone had gone to a lot of trouble to make this video. So I good-naturedly decided to give it a trial run for a few days before moving on to something more challenging.

After the third exercise I literally "hit the wall," then collapsed onto the bed.

Two weeks later, I was still sitting on the bed after the third exercise. I felt mortified, humiliated, demoralized, and devoid of any hope for restored functioning of my arm. Until a nurse friend named Janet walked through the door.

Janet brought a little book titled *14,000 Things to Be Happy About*. She also brought her own story of rehabilitation following her cancer experience. I laughed more than I had in weeks, and by the time she left, I once again had high hopes for my arm. As Janet went out the door, she lifted her arm in a kind of salute, and said, "See? It can be done!"

Walls. I still hated them. But they would never completely stop me again.

Whether the walls serve to commemorate, contain, or challenge, God allows us to hit them. Some will knock us to our knees. But from that lowly position we will look up and hear Him speaking to us.

If we listen, the orders are clear: Go around. Tunnel under. Climb over. Morph through.

Because a grand opportunity awaits us on the other side.

CHAPTER TWENTY

The Dainty China Country

The travelers climbed a ladder to get to the other side of a tall wall. There they discovered a great country made entirely of china. Even the people, animals, and houses were made of china.

To remain on their southern course, the travelers had to cross this china land. As they journeyed they disturbed a china cow, breaking its leg. The china elbow of a milkmaid was also nicked. Everyone in the china land was afraid of being broken except Mr. Joker, the clown. He had been broken so many times he was covered with cracks.

Before they left, one more wall had to be scaled. In jumping the wall, Lion's tail upset a china church and smashed it to pieces.

The travelers were thankful to leave china land behind.

Whether the sufferer moves closer to health or nearer to death, an unforgettable experience called transformation awaits.

> As long as I'm alive in this body, there is good work for me to do. If I had to choose right now, I hardly know which I'd choose. Hard choice! The desire to break camp here and be with Christ is powerful. Some days I can think of nothing better. But most days, because of what you are going through, I am sure that it's better for me to stick it out here.
> —Philippians 1:22–24

Louis writes…

Dear Lord,

I didn't think leaving would be so hard. I like these folks. When I looked in their eyes and told them tomorrow would be my last treatment, I felt like a criminal who had been caught in the act.

When I shared my news, Miss Trish smiled in sort of a sad way and said, "I'm happy for you, Louis. I hope you stay well." Then she closed her eyes and fell asleep.

Little Luke had such a hangdog expression on his face I felt like a total heel for abandoning him. I have to admit, I was disappointed they weren't excited for me.

I'll have to come up with something to bring them both tomorrow…something to remember the Lion's Club. As if we could ever forget any of it.

I'm not sure if I should do what I can to forget all this or try to keep remembering it. Would it make me more thankful for every day if I brought it to mind now and then? Or would it make me feel sad to think about what these people go through?

I have this urge to slam the door on this place tomorrow and never look back. I think deep down I want to forget it ever happened, but I can't do that. So many things have changed…most of them for the better, thanks to You. But thinking about Miss Trish and little Luke will make me sad. How can I forget these people?

The smells of this room, the taste of the chemo in my mouth, the recliners, the intravenous bags, the rides up the elevator, the parking garage, even the exit off the freeway, the nurses, the silly socks, the circus peanuts, the needle sticks… the endless needle sticks. All of it has changed me.

Why me? Why did You allow me to live? I don't know about the others, but my future sounds pretty bright according to Doc. But the whole idea that You may be expecting something from me now scares me, more than just a little bit.

I'm hoping You will let me know whatever it is I'm supposed to be doing with my life. I don't want to seem ungrateful. It would be easy to do some heavy moaning and groaning about how much time I wasted through the years. But that would be senseless, now, wouldn't it?

All for now, I guess.

Amen.

Trisha writes…

Lord,

I just received my last treatment. The cancer has made itself at home…almost everywhere in my body.

Thank You for preparing me for Doc's announcement.

I must be crazy. I'm supposed to be sad, devastated, and angry because You're bringing me home early. But You know what? It doesn't feel early. It feels right. I am ready to move in with You. I'm finally coming home to stay.

Mom and Dad are still here. It will be comforting to have time to enjoy them awhile longer. We can talk about the day when they will move in with You too. Troy and Steven probably have a while to go yet, but I know they will be coming too. I'm going to have to tell Troy where I hid the funeral service list.

I am thankful to have this time with everyone. I hope they will be exceedingly happy for me and only a little bit sad for themselves for a short time.

I hate to ask for anything more from You at this point, Lord. But I am exhausted. If You would either let me sleep on the way to Your house or put me on a jet plane to arrive there faster, I would be truly grateful.

Our Lion Club has been wonderful. How great it is for Louis to go home well. His family will be so pleased. I only wish I could know if little Luke is going to be okay.

I need to stop now. I have to save some energy for Troy and Steven, and Mom and Dad.

See You soon, Father…face to face.
                Amen and love,
                Trisha

Luke writes…

Hi, Jesus!

Mr. Louis is going to be all done with his medisin tomorrow. I think he is happy about it, and so am I. I bet his son Danny Lion is happy too.

Miss Trish was tired again today. I think You need to give her some better medisin. The stuff she's taking isn't helping her. Maybe You should give her the same stuff I have. Mine werks.

Mommy is coming to stay with me when I get my medisin tomorrow. The docter wants to talk to her. I don't like that. Every time he talks to her, it means more needle sticks for me.

I really really really don't like doing my schoolwerk by myself. Please make it so I can go back with the other kids. If Curtis wants to stay in my spot on the teem, he can keep it. Just let me go back and do my werk with the rest of them.

And could You hurry so I won't miss the school carnival?
                Your friend,
                Luke
                Amen.

Something to Think About: Transformations

Webster's New Riverside Dictionary defines *transform* as "to change the nature, function, or condition of."[1] A transformation usually occurs after a sudden awakening. But it may begin by simply peeking through a crack in the curtains to see what's outside.

The act of peeking can be frightening. We don't always like what we see because transformation involves accepting the process of change.

Death is a transformation, a change, and we are conditioned to reject it. But taking a peek at eternal life, and viewing death as a way to reach it, can become an incentive powerful enough to actually welcome the process.

However, peeking takes courage. And some of us don't have the heart of a lion.

Asking some basic questions can help you define your ideas about transformation, death, and eternal life. Do you believe the Bible is the Word of God? If so, do you believe what it says about heaven and how to get there? If so, are you willing to expand your thinking to include viewing your physical body as an outer shell and your inner self as the real you, the part of you that will enjoy eternity?

Through the quiet hours of illness, I gradually came to see my body as the covering for my real self. I likened it to a car's framework. The engine is the heart, the part that allows the car to be driven. My doctors were the mechanics working on my car.

My transformation process began when I lifted the hood of my car and granted God access to do His engine work. It would only be complete when He determined it was necessary to take my car into the shop for the final restoration process, which we call death.

I would no longer need to put gas in my tank, change my oil, or rotate my tires. The "real me" would function smoothly, completing the task for which I was designed—living forever in heaven with my Lord.

I was looking forward to it.

How is your engine running?

---

[1] Webster's II New Riverside Dictionary, Houghton Mifflin Company, 1996, page 714.

CHAPTER TWENTY ONE

The Lion Becomes the King of Beasts

On the other side of the china wall, the travelers discovered a country full of bogs and marshes. They picked their way through it and entered a forest where the trees were big, old, and beautiful. The lion fell in love with it. The beasts of the forest welcomed him as their king, believing he could rescue them from a great spider.

The lion killed the spider while it was sleeping, and the beasts bowed to the lion and worshiped him. He promised to return to them after escorting Dorothy safely on her way to Kansas.

The beasts hiding in forests are not always monsters.

> Be prepared. You're up against far more than you can handle on your own. Take all the help you can get, every weapon God has issued, so that when it's all over but the shouting you'll still be on your feet.
> —Ephesians 6:13

Louis writes…

Dear Lord,
   Well, this is it…the last treatment for the rest of my life. I hope. But this is surely not the last time I will be talking to You.

Never in my wildest dreams did I think I would come to know You like this. Thinking about You, longing to please You, wanting to do things for You. I don't have a clue what I could do that would be worth anything to You, but let me know if You have any ideas, because I'm ready to go.

I imagine I'll be learning a lot as I go to church with Jan and JoEllen. Maybe Michael and his bunch will start going more regularly too. I'm looking forward to talking about You with them. And to seeing the looks on their faces when I do. I'm going to tell Jan that she and I need to start planning a Christmas celebration better than we've ever had before.

I need to get a Bible too. We have a big family one. And Jan has one she uses. But I need my own.

I couldn't figure out what to bring for a good-bye present for Miss Trisha and Luke, so I didn't bring anything. It turns out I didn't need to worry about either one of them.

Trisha didn't show up today. I'm not too surprised. She was looking pretty peaked yesterday.

And Luke's mom came with him today. I'd feel sort of silly playing the Lion Club with her around.

I'm around the last of this bag drip through my veins. When all this started, I didn't believe I would ever get out of here. I guess You could say I was lacking in the faith department. But You made a believer out of me. You've given me the world back and I didn't even know I had lost it until the word *cancer* was written across my chart.

Here comes the doc. Wonder what he wants now. He's talking to Luke's mom and she's smiling big time. Must be good news…

It was *great* news. Luke is being released too. Tomorrow is his last treatment. You can't beat that for great timing.

I'd better pick up something on my way home this afternoon and bring it in tomorrow. That boy will have ants in his pants trying to sit through the last bag and he'll need something to distract him.

The Lion Becomes the King of Beasts

Thanks, Lord! Amen! And Amen again! Two of our lions are being set free.

Now, how about giving our lady lioness a hand up?

Trisha writes...

Jesus,

My family is tiptoeing around me. They all have red eyes with bags under them. I almost look better than they do. They seem to be avoiding me. Help me be patient.

I know it's not easy for them. I remember how I felt before I knew You this well. Death was almost spooky. It meant a separation from everything known. But now, after You have taken me through so much...after You have stood at my side...after You have let me see so much of You...all I can think about is going home and being with You.

If I said these words to anyone, they would probably gasp or shake their heads. I think my family wants me to fight, to hold on, or to try something else to get rid of the cancer. They were all upset when I refused to go in for treatment today.

But I know my earthly work is finished. One last thing I'd like to do is have one more visit with little Luke. So if You wouldn't mind, please give me the strength to make it up there tomorrow. I've been saving something for him and Louis.

After that...well, I just want to go home and curl up in Your arms for eternity.

Okay?

Trish

Luke writes...

Dear Jesus,

You are just the best! I've been asking You to let me go back to school, and You said okay!

One more day! Docter says just *one more day!* I wish Miss Trish was here so I could tell her the news. Maybe tomorrow she'll be back. I know she would come if she knew it was my *last day!*

I hope I can sleep tonight so the wait won't seem so long.
Amen!

Something to Think About: Last Days

If you knew you would die tomorrow, what would you be doing today?

A person who has escaped a life-threatening illness may answer that question differently than those who have never had the experience. Facing death, whether through illness or danger, heightens awareness of the commonplace, the ordinary, the simple, sweet pleasures of everyday life. Having family or friends who are willing to be pulled into the experience adds to the enchantment of peering at death while enjoying life.

As we strive to be transformed into the image of Christ, we become more sensitive to the needs of those around us. Such needs can be overwhelming if we take our eyes off our Savior. The words of Paul encourage us:

> No prolonged infancies among us, please. We'll not tolerate babes in the woods, small children who are an easy mark for impostors. God wants us to grow up, to know the whole truth and tell it in love—like Christ in everything. We take our lead from Christ, who is the source of everything we do. He keeps us in step with each other. His very breath and blood flow through us, nourishing us so that we will grow up healthy in God, robust in love.
> —Ephesians 4:14–16

Robust-in-love means shedding tears and drying them. It means holding a hand and letting go of a hand. It means having tea when you would rather have coffee. It means rubbing a back when your own needs to be rubbed.

What would you be doing today if you knew you would die tomorrow?

God's *robust-in-love* answer is "I would be doing exactly what I'm doing right now."

CHAPTER TWENTY TWO

The Country of the Quadlings

After the travelers passed through the forest, they came to a steep hill covered with sharp rocks. They began to climb it, but were stopped by strange men with heads like rubber bands, which stretched and snapped, flinging Scarecrow aside. Dorothy called on the winged monkeys to carry them over the hill. It was the last time she could summon their help. They wished her goodbye and good luck.

The travelers took the road to the South, where a young girl met them. The girl asked the good witch, Glinda, to receive them. They were admitted at once into the castle.

Lifting a boulder together, be it heavy or light, is always uniting when the lift is accomplished for the same purpose.

Enter with the password: "Thank you!" Make yourselves at home, talking praise. Thank him. Worship him.
—Psalm 100:4

Louis writes…

Dear Lord,
Please make this elevator hurry up and open its doors. I just want to get up there, drop off this stuffed lion for little

Luke, and sail out of here. This place really bugs me now that I don't have to be here.

Finally! Nobody else is in the elevator. Good.

I got in and pressed the button. But somebody's arm stopped the door from closing.

"Can you please hold it for me just a minute?" a middle-aged man asked. He stepped back to help someone walk in.

"Sure." I guessed I shouldn't be too contrary.

The couple entered. The man supported a woman who was all hunched over. She had a big red nylon bag slung over her shoulder.

No. Dear God, please don't tell me...

The man punched the button for their floor and she looked up. Her face white as bone china, her eyes dark as swamp water. It was her.

"The lioness has come to deliver one more mission. Completed it only this morning." She smiled softly and spoke even more softly. "Aren't you supposed to be finished with your treatments?"

"I am. But little Luke is having his last one today, so I thought I'd bring him this stuffed lion to distract him."

"He's finished too?" Her pale eyes showed some life for a brief moment.

I nodded. Hard to believe a person could deteriorate so quickly. She wouldn't even be standing if her husband wasn't holding her.

She looked up at him. "You know, Troy," she whispered, "I think it would be better for the other official member of the Lion Club to deliver this final mission. The lioness only needed to know the cub was going to be fine. I know now, and I'd just like to go back home. Okay?"

Troy held out a sack. Inside was a big box wrapped in gold paper.

I took the sack. "I'd be glad to make the delivery for the lioness."

"There's something in the box for you too. I was going to leave it with the nurse to give you when you came in

The Country of the Quadlings

next." She struggled to speak a little louder. "I want to say thanks. I'm proud to be part of your pride."

"The feeling is mutual, Miss Trish." I swallowed hard. "We couldn't have done it without you."

"You've almost got it right," she said hoarsely. "We couldn't have done it without *Him*."

The elevator door opened to our floor. I stepped out, sack in hand, and turned back to meet her eyes. She smiled, leaning back into her husband's arms. As the doors closed on our lioness, the lump in my throat nearly strangled me.

I lifted the box from the sack. She had written on it: *For two very brave Lion Kings from their Lioness.*

I reverently removed the lid from the box and lifted out two golden crowns. One large and one small. Leaning against the wall, I slumped to the floor.

Box in one hand, crowns in the other, I bawled like a baby.

Luke writes…

Dear Jesus,

I am almost done. Yay! Mr. Louis came by with a toy lion for me, and he had a mission delivery from Miss Trish. It was crowns for us two Lion Kings. Mr. Louis said we were so strong now that we each needed to start our own prides wherever we live.

So that's what I'm going to do. If I cant play soccer at recess, then I'll get some guys to be in my pride.

Thanks for the crowns and the toy lion and for Miss Trish and Mr. Louis and for getting me back to my school next Monday. I will try to be the best lion You ever had, even better than the ones on Noah's big boat.

See you later, Jesus! Keep all them angels singing good!

Love and amen!
Your friend,
Luke

Something to Think About: More Time

"Honey, wake up! Talk to me!" my aunt shouted over her shoulder to her husband's inert form lying in the backseat of the car.

JoAnn drove to the hospital as fast as she dared, alternately calling out encouragements and listening for movements and breathing from the backseat. Her mind swarmed with memories, scenes flitting in and out of her consciousness as she vowed to conquer this latest obstacle in her husband's battle with cancer.

"We'll make it to the hospital in time. They'll fix whatever's wrong with your breathing. Then we'll go home, where you can get a good night's sleep in your own bed. We'll wake up tomorrow morning, have some breakfast, and laugh about this crazy night." She wasn't sure if she was trying to convince him or herself.

A stoplight turned red. "Why, God, why?" She looked both ways, saw no traffic, and gunned the car through the intersection.

"How are you doing back there, honey?" No response. "We're nearly to the parking lot. Take a deep breath. We're gonna make it!"

She careened under the emergency entrance canopy, bringing the car to a quick halt. She jumped out, laying on the horn to summon help. As she waited for the ER crew to come out, she opened the back door and bent down to take her husband's face in her hands.

"Honey, we're here." Tears surged down her cheeks. Through the watery veil, she memorized the look on his face, each crease, each line. She noted the folds at the corners of his mouth, hinting at a smile. She ran her fingers over his eyebrows, her lips over his cheeks. And she felt the conspicuous absence of his breath. An abrupt, painful awareness shot through her heart like ripples on a pond.

Gently, she cradled his head to her chest and whispered the words resonating through every corner of her mind. "I thought we had more time."

Each moment, each hour, every day, week, month, and year is a gift from our loving and gracious God. Two things are crucial to using time to its fullest measure.

First, we must be certain we belong to God. We need to be convinced that we are His children, that He is our Father. We can glean assurance of this fact from the truths of Scripture. "If you confess with your mouth, 'Jesus is Lord,' and believe in your heart that God raised him from the dead, you will be saved" (Romans 10:9 NIV).

God wants each of us in heaven, and He's made it so plain and simple that a child can understand. Trusting in His words brings life everlasting, a heavenly future guaranteed.

Second, we must be convinced that God has an intense interest in how we live our lives from day to day. As we reach this level of awareness, God speaks to us continually through the work of the Holy Spirit, through the Bible, through prayer, circumstances, and other believers. As we undergo the process of spiritual growth, we are led to a wonderful climactic experience when we realize our length of time spent on earth is a gift to be shared, not a chore to be endured. We learn to listen to His voice, enjoying our freedom as He guides us through each twist and turn of life.

When family members or friends are taken from us, we grieve. We long to know why. We may even demand that God tell us His entire plan. We raise our fists to heaven and cry, "Why didn't You tell me this was going to happen?"

Yet while we mourn the loss of earthly time, we can anticipate a heavenly future…where time will be insignificant, where all that matters is being with Him.

"I thought we had more time" can become "Thank You for the time we had."

CHAPTER TWENTY THREE

Glinda Grants Dorothy's Wish

Dorothy told Glinda of her wish to return home to Kansas. She told Dorothy the silver shoes on her feet had the power to carry her back home. Dorothy discovered she could have gone home on the very first day she arrived in the strange country. The silver shoes could carry her anywhere she wished, if she would only knock the heels together three times and speak her command.

Dorothy's fellow travelers were glad she hadn't known this, for they would have missed out on receiving their wishes.

Dorothy said her good-byes, picked up her dog, clicked her heels, and said, "Take me home to Aunt Em!" Her wish was granted.

The shoes were lost in flight.

A home heaped with love is made invincible with exquisitely painful farewells.

> But friends, that's exactly who we are: children of God. And that's only the beginning. Who knows how we'll end up! What we know is that when Christ is openly revealed, we'll see him—and in seeing him, become like him. All of us who look forward to his Coming stay ready, with the glistening purity of Jesus' life as a model for our own.
>
> —1 John 3:2–3

Trisha's mom writes…

"Mom?" I heard my daughter say.

"I'm here, honey," I assured her. "What do you need?"

I tenderly leaned over her shiny, perspiring head and wiped her brow gently. How I wished I could make this easier for her.

"I don't need a thing. I have had absolutely everything good this world could give." Her voice, scratchy and rough, strained as she spoke. "I think it's nearly time for me to go home. I've been here long enough."

"I think so, too, honey." With tears pouring down my cheeks, I asked, "Do you want me get your guys and Daddy?"

"That would be great." As I stood, she called me back. "Mom, there's one more thing. I always wanted to be like you, you know? Trying to do it all just right. But I didn't get to see you do…this. So I'm not sure I'm doing it right." She paused to catch her breath. "What do you think? Am I doing a halfway decent job?"

My voice caught in my throat. "You are doing a superb job, my precious daughter. Much better than I could ever do." I paused to catch my breath. "Now I will have to try to do it right, just like you."

She grinned feebly. "Oh, Mom."

"Hold on, sweetie. Let me go get the fellows." I left hastily, not wanting to miss a single, fleeting second with her.

Troy, Steven, and Dad stood from the kitchen table as soon as they saw my face. I motioned them to follow.

Troy kneeled beside her bed and took her hand. "Trish?"

"Hey, honey."

"You okay? Do you hurt anywhere?"

"I am so fine you wouldn't believe it." Her voice was raspy as she tried to laugh. "But you won't be fine if you can't find the funeral service instructions."

"Aw, Trish, stop. I love you so much it hurts."

"I love you too. But it doesn't hurt at all. I'll see you in about forty or fifty years, okay? It'll go fast. I promise." She closed her eyes.

Troy pulled her hand to his mouth, holding it in a kiss.

She lifted her free hand and beckoned to her son. "Steven?"

With face ready to crumple, our courageous twelve-year-old grabbed her hand like a lifeline. "I'm here, Mom," he said. "How are you doin'?"

"I am ready to go on this trip. I can hardly wait. And I want you to do something for me."

"Anything."

"All these wonderful people here in this room are going to want to be sad when I leave."

"Me, too, Mom." His young voice cracked with emotion.

"It's okay to be sad for a little while, but not too long. Don't let them be sad too long. Because I'm not going to be sad. I'm going to be having the time of my life."

He leaned over and kissed her on the cheek.

"You remember all those Bible stories I read to you about heaven?"

"Uh-huh."

"They're true. Every one of them. And it's even more beautiful than the pictures. Do you understand?"

"I've got it, Mom."

She swallowed hard as he let go of her hand and stepped away from her side. "Dad?"

My hurting husband stood at the foot of the bed and squeezed her toes. "Right here, baby."

"Suppose I could trouble you for one last sip of that cool water you're always bringing me?" Her voice, growing weaker with each breath, barely spoke the words out loud.

But because he was a father who listened carefully, he heard every word. He reached for the glass that he had proudly kept filled to the top with ice and fresh water through each day and night of her illness. Gently, slowly, with love in every tiny movement, he tipped the glass to her lips.

She drank. "Thanks, Daddy. That hit the spot. I'll be taking off on my trip now."

"Godspeed, Daughter. Godspeed."

CHAPTER TWENTY FOUR

Home Again

A unt Em looked up and saw Dorothy running toward her. She folded the little girl into her arms, covering her with kisses.

Running into open arms is the best part about coming home.

May God himself, the God who makes everything holy and whole, make you holy and whole, put you together—spirit, soul, and body—and keep you fit for the coming of our Master, Jesus Christ. The One who called you is completely dependable. If he said it, he'll do it!
—1 Thessalonians 5:23–24

Trisha writes…

> I see the gates. They're wide open. Everything is so bright and beautiful!
> And there He is…waiting for me. Just like He said He would be.
> "Father! It's me! I'm finally here!"
> As I fling myself into His waiting arms, He says, "Welcome home, Trisha. Welcome home."

Good-bye, friends.
Love mixed with faith be yours
from God the Father and from the Master, Jesus Christ.
Pure grace and nothing but grace
be with all who love our Master, Jesus Christ.
—Ephesians 6:23–24

When Words Fail, Pray

The moment we get tired in the waiting, God's Spirit is right alongside helping us along. If we don't know how or what to pray, it doesn't matter. He does our praying in and for us, making prayer out of our wordless sighs, our aching groans.... That's why we can be so sure that every detail in our lives of love for God is worked into something good.
—Romans 8:26–28

Dear Reader,

When facing great challenges in life, most of us experience such a depth of pain that we believe no one can possibly understand how we feel. For this reason, I am sharing some of the prayers I prayed while traveling my road "From Kansas to Oz." I hope they will serve to let you know that others have walked your road and known your distress.

You are not alone. I will continue to pray for *you*...that your days will be filled with an ever-increasing awareness of God's presence and that your nights will bring you His restorative, healing peace.

In His love,
Gail Larson

Oh, God,

The tears are coming again. I know in my heart You have a wonderful place prepared for me—more awesome than anything I could ever imagine. But still I long to see more of my life's days on this earth. Help me savor each moment here, as I learn to hunger for heaven.

Give me words to make my family strong. Give me faith to endure this fiery furnace in which I live. Give me strength to accept Your good and perfect will.

For Jesus' sake. Amen.

Dear Lord,

You gave me this body. And You are allowing a part of it to be taken away.

My heart grieves for this loss. As the time grows closer to make the separation, I can find no words to make me feel better. So hear my sighs and my cries, and help me thank You for the time I was given to use this wonderful piece of myself.

Give me courage to adapt to life without it. I can stand up in front of the world with You by my side...no matter how I look.

In Your name I plead, amen.

Dear Lord,

What a body You have given me! Forgive me for all the years I took it for granted. Keep reminding me of Your presence in all facets of my illness. Let the journey down this dark road be brightened by many little victories. Show me how to enjoy each triumph.

Surround me with understanding caregivers who will allow me the privilege of sharing losses and celebrating successes. Thank You for never leaving my side.

In Your supportive name I pray, amen.

Dear Lord,

I wish You would tell me exactly how much time I have left. If I knew for sure, I'd like to think I would use the time better. That I would be nicer. That I would get to know You more.

Forgive me for wasting Your precious gift of life. Give me courage to break down walls of my own making, to say words that heal, words that convey love.

Let me spend life as You choose, not as I choose. I extravagantly spend the time You give me by wondering…wondering how heaven's going to look, wondering if You'll really let me in, if I'll see anyone I know, if my family will miss me.

Teach me instead to wonder at the immensity of life, to stand in awe of Your gift of salvation, and to share the good news of Jesus with everyone. Thank You, Lord, for giving me time to know You. For Jesus' sake. Amen.

Dear Lord,

I have seen this same road too many times. Hasn't it been long enough?

I'm trying to make the most of this road trip on which You've sent me, but I'm tired of traveling. I long for a road with no potholes.

Help me appreciate the journey. Remind me that every earthly road will have bumps, detours, and ruts. Show me how to look past the challenges of a rough ride to see You, to see the broad, smooth expanse of Your heaven beckoning me forward.

Make heaven real for me, Lord. Make it be more than words on a page. Let it be the reason I can face another trip down this same road tomorrow.

For Jesus' sake, I ask You. Amen.

Lord of Acapulco, chemotherapy, and oasis bags,

I thank You for allowing me to live in a time when a diagnosis of cancer brings hope and possibilities. With so many new treatment frontiers, I know You are engineering gifted men and women to bring healing in a variety of ways. In the midst of tests and diagnoses, help me remember the source of healing is You.

When I open my oasis bag, let Your Holy Spirit jump out and reenergize my relationship with You. Let this time of chemotherapy be a time to experience Your presence in all of its love, comfort, and hope.

Lord, thank You for the simple joys my oasis bag brings to me and others. Maybe You'll let me take it to Acapulco someday?

With much anticipation for the days ahead, I am very thankful to be Your child. Amen.

Dear God,

At this moment, I don't feel as if I'm winning any battles. I know the fight is supposed to help me grow, but I really don't want to do it like this. I want everything to go back to the way it was before.

Show me how to yearn for the growth that You want for me. Show me how to cope with the battle my body is enduring. Teach me to be like You in every obstacle I encounter. For Your sake, I ask. Amen.

Lord,

I ache for the day when I will feel strong again. I covet the energy You once gave me and I resent seeing it ooze out of everyone around me. Why can't I have some of it?

If I had more energy, I'd be shaking my fist at You, demanding that You give it back.

Look inside my mind, God…because that's what I'm doing right now. I don't see the point of all this. Maybe I never will. Yet somehow, You still love me. And for this moment, it is enough. For Jesus' sake. Amen.

Dear God,

Thank You for being almighty. Thank You for being all powerful. Thank You for controlling even the cells in my body. I know You love me and will use the weakness of my illness to draw me closer to You. I look forward to knowing You deeper than before.

You are the reason I can fight this battle. And because You say "fight," I will fight….to triumph, not just endure. In Your life-giving, life-saving name, I pray. Amen.

About the Author

Gail Larson is an accomplished storyteller and word artist. She captures the hearts and emotions of her readers with her true-to-life stories painted from personal experience.

She is the founder of Larson Ministries. Its mission is "Making God's Word real for you." Her stories and spiritual seminars support this goal by motivating, strengthening, and encouraging a daily renewal of faith for all. To learn more about Larson Ministries, or to schedule Gail Larson to speak to your group, go to www.larsonministries.com.

Red tote bags, like the one mentioned in this book, are available for purchase. Gail's original "oasis bag" was a gift from the hospital where her journey with cancer started. She began carrying it to appointments and chemotherapy treatments. She filled it with necessities for her physical comfort and also included items that brought her joy and hope. These tote bags are red with black trim and a silhouette of a palm tree.

To Order Your Oasis Bag

Visit

www.myoasisbag.com

To order additional copies of

From Kansas to OZ

Have your credit card ready and call

Toll free: (877) 421-READ (7323)

or order online at: www.winepressbooks.com